Blood Debts

Clan of Shadows #1.5

C.D. Britt

PHOENYX PUBLISHING, LLC.

Phoenyx Publishing, LLC.

Please be advised this book touches on these topics:

- Domestic violence

- Death

- Drinking of blood (there be vampires)

- Matricide (killing of husband)

- Uxoricide (killing of wife)

- Buried (well, dead, but came back to life) alive

- Suicide (off page)

- lack of women's reproductive rights (medieval equivalent of plan B obtained. Don't worry, loves.)

Contents

Terms

Chieftain – leader of a Túath.

Túath – tribe.

Túatha De Danann – tribe of Danu, gods and goddesses of the Irish Pantheon, tribe of gods, and folk of the goddess Danu.

Dearg Due – first female vampire.

Sluagh – unforgiven dead that prey on the souls of the living.

Danu – mother goddess of the Túatha De Danann.

The Morrigan – goddess of war and fate.

Playlist

The Unwanted Animal by The Amazing Devil
Labour by Paris Paloma
Bluebird by Meg Myers
Another Love (Violin) Dramatic Violin
Hunter (the cacophony) by Paris Paloma
Bite Marks by League of Legends & TEYA
Burn your village by Kiki Rockwell
Too Much by Dove Cameron
How Villains Are Made by Madalen Duke
Unsweetened Lemonade by Amélie Farren
Dangerous Woman by Tom Evans
Here I am by Tommee Profitt, Brooke
Bears & Wolves by Lilith Max
Don't Cry for your Daughters Eve by Lydia the Bard
Peasant's Throne by Lilith Max
The Fruits by Paris Paloma

To the women who are still fighting.
Don't stop. Don't yield. Don't retreat.
Stand strong.

Chapter 1

LATE MIDDLE AGES - IRELAND

Niamh moved the potatoes around on her plate, her eyes focused on the swirl in the dark red sauce, ignoring the booming voices.

Despite the lively atmosphere of the Waterford castle dinners—a mix of clinking silverware, whispers, and distant music—no one spoke to her.

She was the wife of the new Lord, all a part of the recent changes the men from across the channel brought with them.

Now, they were no longer a Túath with a Chieftain like Niamh had grown up with. They were now a city with a castle and a man of the peerage. Once the new Lord of Waterford had taken power, her father had jumped at the chance to sell her off.

If the men in their longboats didn't revolutionize things, the men from across the channel did.

Niamh almost wished the barbaric men in their longboats had still been around. At least they were less pretentious and were not cluttering the landscape with the circular towers built to house monks of a new and less inclusive religion. A religion whose rigid doctrines left women little solace.

Each night was the same. She pushed the food around on her plate until dismissed to get ready for bed, praying for her husband to leave her alone.

Niamh shivered against the chill from the stone walls. Even with the fires lit, the room was far too big for the small flames to heat the monstrosity. She pulled her wool shawl tighter, the emerald silk gown her husband had bought for her doing nothing against the cold.

Across the long wooden table, lined with the elite of her little spot in the world, was her husband, large and imposing. Even in his cups, he did not loosen at all. Instead, hands folded in front of his face, his dark eyes watched and took in the conversations around them.

Secrets she knew he would use to manipulate. He would gain favor with some, blackmail others, and ultimately pass an unfair law in the Irish House of Lords. A law that would hurt the very people he was supposed to protect.

The very stone walls that ensconced their burgeoning little city were protection to some, but a prison for her.

No, the stone walls around her were not her home. Neither was the land she'd grown up on, now with plenty of livestock to show her father's new gains after bartering off his only daughter against her mother's wishes.

The day Niamh married, her mother had died of a broken heart, knowing her darling girl was walking down the road to the same fate as her.

"Lord Gwyer discussing an heir must be exciting for you!"

Niamh's head shot up at the words whispered to her from the woman beside her, one she didn't even bother to get to know. Niamh's husband rarely allowed her freedom to choose her own friends, even of the people he surrounded her with. All but one. But she was Lord Gwyer's oldest friend's wife, so he made an allowance and allowed Niamh to have a friendship with her.

Lady Shaw, was the vapid woman speaking, her older husband next to her in his finest overcoat, making do with the means they had while his wife wore a dark gray woolen dress, a tad too tight for her, with a covetous eye on Niamh's gown.

"I beg your pardon?" Niamh finally spoke, realizing it was the first words she had uttered all evening.

The woman gasped with berry red lips far overdone, her hand going to her pale chest that spilled out of her dress, in shock at Niamh's words.

Pretentious.

"Why, all evening he boasted soon Waterford will have an heir!"

From across the candlelit table, Niamh's eyes met her husband's; his gaze was direct, and his expression unreadable.

She wasn't pregnant, a fact that filled her with a desperate, aching relief as she silently pleaded with any god listening to keep it that way. To bring a child into her nightmare made Niamh want to walk into the lake and let the lady have her.

"Chieftain Gwyer speaks out of turn," Niamh whispers back and the narrowed look Lady Shaw gave her had her curling her fingers around her fork.

Lady Shaw repeated, "He needs an heir," implying that her failure to provide one immediately made her a failure in their new society's eyes.

Niamh's stomach turned.

"Perhaps he can find one in the slums his greedy laws and corrupt practices created."

The chatter near Niamh stopped, an unsettling hush falling over the room as her husband's gaze sharpened, fixing on her.

He knew she was not one to bend easily, and that was why he took his hand to her almost every day. Yet, she had not broken in spirit, and that was fine with him, since he seemed to enjoy the challenge.

They were all like that, the entire group of new Lords and Ladies, and she despised surrendering to the avarice and malevolence of others by saying nothing when they spoke; the sheer pettiness of it all grated on her nerves.

One day, while they were sipping the wine made from the labor of others, she'd slip something into it. She would put an end to the horrifying, nightmarish new reality that had become her life.

And when she danced on his grave, she would see them, all the people under his heavy hand, free of the demon at last.

"Perhaps this is not the time or place to speak of such things," Lord Shaw intervened and Niamh felt a small bit of warmth toward the man. One of the few who did not act as if their new titles gave them free rein to make others suffer.

Niamh pondered if he felt as trapped as she did. If perhaps they all did and just danced around that discomfort to avoid facing the emptiness inside them.

Her eyes lifted and met with Lady Agnew's ice blue ones. The only other person at the table who truly knew Niamh. Cae's blonde hair formed a crown around her head, and she wore a dark blue silk dress embroidered almost as beautiful as her own.

The only other soul in the entire room that understood Niamh. Lady Agnew, Cae, nodded to Niamh before looking down again, her husband one of the few people from their old life, before Niamh's husband became a lord.

The silence of her meal was heavy with the bitterness of missing her friend. Each bite tasted like ash in her mouth.

A whipping wind blew through the room, causing the candles to flicker and the tapestries to snap. Servants rushed to fix what had fallen.

Which was odd, since the doors were closed.

The other guests exchanged uneasy glances and subtle smirks. Their silent curiosity was palpable, but not enough to curtail the evening's festivities, and so Niamh continued her silent suffering.

Chapter 2

Niamh made it through dinner, but she knew what was coming when the night was at its witching hour. After he'd indulged in more of the wine and whiskey, he'd be in a vicious mood, and Niamh always felt the worst of his wrath on nights like this.

Making her way to her rooms, a hand grabbed her elbow, pulling her into one of the guest rooms. The door she had stood outside of for several nights, wishing she were the one lying with Lady Agnew instead of her dreadful husband.

As the lips of her paramour found hers in the darkened room, a wave of passionate longing washed over Niamh; the kiss was a welcome release after a night of forced politeness to repulsive people. The closeness of their bodies was a delicious contrast to her earlier discomfort. Arousal and lust filled the air as she took her lover's bottom lip between her teeth, stealing small kisses before trailing her lips down the length of her lover's throat. Niamh indulged herself in the fleeting pleasure, its memory a sweet burden to carry through the long night.

Pulling back before Niamh lost herself completely and someone walked in, she laid her forehead against Cae's. The mirror in the room reflected their embrace in a hazy glow as Niamh burned the image into her memory. Niamh was taller, her black hair a stark contrast to her pale skin, her dark eyes almost black.

But Cae was the light to Niamh's darkness with her blonde beauty and sun-tanned skin.

"An heir, Niamh?" Cae whispered, her hands moving along Niamh's curved waist.

Swallowing down the words she wanted to say, to beg, she shook her head.

"Not if I can help it. I will not give that man another life to torment."

Nodding, Cae kissed the hollow of Niamh's throat before she stepped back. "Then come with me tomorrow. Outside of the market... that is where I procure a tincture to avoid finding myself with child."

Footsteps moved toward where they were in the hallway, and Niamh knew her lady's maid, such a ridiculous concept, would be in her room in a matter of minutes.

With a last, lingering kiss, she nodded. Cae slipped Niamh a small, folded piece of paper, its edges slightly browned and smelling faintly of fresh ink; a note of poetry and promises, one Niamh knew she would immediately burn after reading. The thought of keeping them, however much Niamh desired it, would only fuel her husband's rage if he found them, leaving her with aching bruises and a battered spirit.

"Tomorrow we can ride out while the men hunt," Niamh whispered against Cae's lips. The warmth of her breaths a fleeting sensation, before pulling her into a brief hug before letting her go.

Niamh's heart pounded against her ribs as she slipped into the hall and checked for onlookers before retreating to her chambers.

As she entered her room, hiding Cae's love note in her bodice since she had no pockets, she found she wasn't alone. Her heart pounded as she closed the door, wondering how much her lady's maid had seen.

"My lady," Babette, her lady's maid, gave a small curtsy.

"You are quick, Babette." Niamh whispered, but as her eyes acclimated in the low candlelight of her room, she could see the fear in Babette's eyes. "But you didn't have far to travel, did you?"

Babette flinched. Her gloved hand shot up, covering the angry purple bruises on her neck. They were shaped like Lord Gwyer's fingers, stark against her pale skin. "I was..."

Stepping toward her, Niamh's gaze sharpened, but she quickly softened her expression so Babette wouldn't feel threatened. "You are not to excuse him for his behavior. He was born to create hell on earth. We are but the innocents fed to the demon to appease him and keep him from harming the ones with the power to stop him."

Babette dropped her hand, folding them in front of her, her head down. "Yes, my lady. Would you like me to help you get ready for bed?"

Even Niamh could hear the resignation in her lady's maid's voice. It seemed her husband would join her tonight. They both knew if Niamh did not attend to her wifely duties, there would be hell for the entire household to pay.

As it did most nights, the words, "pack me a bag," trembled on the edge of her tongue, a desperate plea Niamh suppressed. The words weighed down on her, making it hard to breathe.

And yet, despite the rising fear that choked her, she remained silent. Niamh would see none of those in her employ lost to his wrath from her actions. In the entirety of her life, Niamh had little control; yet she could control her actions toward her husband to save those around her from his poisonous retribution.

"Yes, please, but also, tomorrow I will join Cae on a trip to the market. I need some fresh air not addled by pompous men and their demands."

Babette, with a silent nod, moved to assist Niamh in shedding the constricting silk dress, the whisper of the fabric filling the quiet room.

Niamh missed her simple wool dresses. Their comforting texture was a stark contrast to the silks and furs her husband made her wear, making her feel like a prized mare on display.

With deft hands, Babette eased Niamh out of her gown, the scent of lavender and linen filling the air.

Niamh seized the opportunity to remove the note as Babette put the dress away, but Niamh had not been quick enough.

"He would see you dead for carrying on with this affair, my lady." The fear in Babette's voice shook Niamh, and Niamh understood if her husband found out they were both as good as dead. Babette was far too loyal to Niamh for her husband to keep around for the next Lady Gwyer.

Gently placing the note in the antique drawer of her ornate dressing table, she turned to face her lady's maid, whose chapped hands she clasped in her own. "I am being as careful as I can, but he wishes an heir, and I just need to get out of this house to see that nothing comes of this. Do you understand?"

A silent agreement passed between them as Babette nodded, her fingers tightening around Niamh's hands. She knew what Niamh felt from the many nights she had spilled her worries to Babette. When she begged Babette to make excuses for Niamh so she could stay out of his sight when the moon called for a child.

But with the moon's cycle aligning with her husband's visit, the weight of her impending pregnancy pressed down on her, feeling inescapable now.

Babette let out a long, weary sigh, the sound echoing softly in the quiet room as she turned Niamh to finish her laces. As she did so, Niamh looked at herself in the mirror, but did not see anything but a vessel for a rich man's heir.

Her lady maid's hands moved gently as she helped her into the silken nightgown, the soft fabric a whisper against her bare skin, yet her thoughts remained distant and troubled.

All her life, she had been a prize, a bargaining chip, for those who should have seen her as a person, even before the men across the channel brought the new religion over. A time when a woman had plenty of rights, but Niamh was nothing more than her father's tool for negotiating himself a fortune.

If only she could erase herself from this life. To disappear into the darkness where no one could find her.

And if they somehow did, well, then she would find herself the predator instead of the prey.

Perhaps with Cae at her side.

Her heart hammered a wild tattoo against her ribs at the mere thought of her love. Her hand flew to her chest to feel the frantic beat, and a wave of delicious heat washed over her as memories returned.

Cae had visited the new Waterford Estate with her husband three years after Niamh had wed Lord Gwyer. Niamh knew Cae had seen the quiet desperation in her eyes. She had seen the way Niamh moved through the house like a ghost and offered her a lifeline of friendship and unwavering support. A gift that Niamh returned with the whole of herself.

Soon, Cae had become more, and the afternoon tea soon included stolen kisses. Niamh's cheeks flushed as she thought of the forays to the country that had become long nights of lovemaking in the forest, like the nymphs of old. How they had spent their days daydreaming of escaping their husbands and running away with each other. They dreamed of a secluded woodland cottage, a refuge from life's troubles, where they could grow old together. Where Niamh would finally know what a home full of love felt like. One where she could be her true self.

Excitement at the very thought burned through Niamh before the feeling of hopelessness robbed her of it. A suffocating tightness gripped her lungs, her eyes stinging with unshed tears, yet Niamh forced her eyes closed, determined to keep the depression at bay.

In a society that would devour them, their love was a dangerous, beautiful fantasy that consumed her soul. To Niamh, being with Cae was worth any risk, even death, but Cae refused to take that step until she could guarantee their safety.

With a squeeze to Niamh's shoulders, Babette pulled her from her thoughts, and Niamh sat at her dressing table for Babette to brush through Niamh's midnight tresses. Thinking of the note in the top drawer for her to read, she tried to hold on to the courage she knew she would need to make it through the evening.

Tomorrow promised her time with her love and a solution to the problem that was her husband desiring an heir.

At least for now.

Chapter 3

Niamh pulled on her heavy woolen cloak, the rough fabric a stark contrast to her cotton dress. She stepped towards the open door where a servant waited, the ornate carriage to town gleaming in the sunlight.

The comforting weight of her wool cloak, heavy and warm, and the soft cotton of her favorite blue dress, a memory of simpler times, brought a sense of comfort. The feeling of who she was before she became the Lady of Waterford.

Her husband had come late in the night, but with her plan to prevent pregnancy in place, she could get through the feel of his hands on her skin. Of his rough thrusts and quick climax that left her feeling like nothing more than something quick to dispose. Once done, he put back on his robe and stood to leave, just as he did every night that they were intimate.

But this time, he was not silent as he opened the door before slipping away into the night.

"If you are not pregnant in a fortnight, I will expect more from you. Two or three times a week will not be enough."

Niamh shivered as she ran her hands up and down her arms, the thought more chilling than the winter air making its way in for the season.

Tadhg, her beloved horse, was one of the two horses taking her into town. She was quick to walk around as she waited for Cae in order to sneak him a treat she had pilfered from the kitchens during breakfast that morning.

Niamh laughed as his lips rolled in anticipation as she held her hand out, and Tadhg gently nipped, taking the treat without a single finger lost. Her gentle giant.

"Today," she spoke as if sharing a secret with her horse. "We will visit someone new to help us." Tadhg let out a sweet nicker and rubbed his face against her neck and shoulder.

Oh, how she wished she could wear pants. That she could feel the wind in her hair as she sat astride Tadhg, just like the men did. Just like she used to in her youth when her father left for Túath business.

"Wife."

A sudden, sharp breath escaped Niamh's lips as she froze, her heart hammering in her chest. Turning, she stepped around Tadhg to the other side of the carriage to face her husband.

Nodding to the footman that waited by the carriage, her husband turned and eyed her as she straightened her shoulders.

"I looked for you in your rooms." As usual, he stood tall and silent, his jaw clenched tight, a storm brewing behind his eyes. He'd let her puzzle over his mood, his silence heavy with the unspoken question of whether he was truly angry. She never knew, and with the curious eyes of an audience upon them, she wouldn't until they were alone later.

"Yes, Lady Agnew and I were planning to go into town for a little shopping." Just enough information to look like a wife simply wanting to spend the unearned money of her wealthy husband.

His eyes narrowed. "I would prefer you stay here until you are with child."

Niamh's hands shook as she clasped them in front of her. When he was in one of his moods, he would trap her within the stone walls, keeping her from visiting or having visitors. If she were with child, she could only imagine how he would behave.

No, she needed to make sure that it never happened.

"I understand, my lord, but perhaps I could have this one day to visit the markets with my friend before we focus on such a thing."

"Ah! Lord Gwyer! Just the gent I was looking for!"

Niamh could have kissed her husband's solicitor at that moment. There was no way her husband would say no with someone of such importance watching. Lord Gwyer was all about projecting the face of a perfect husband and lord in front of others who could carry his immaculate reputation back to the king.

With an air of superiority, he nodded to the solicitor. "I was just seeing my wife off."

Without another word or glance in her direction, he walked with the solicitor toward the front doors. His words were full of the sickly charm he used on those who didn't know the demon beneath the skin.

Niamh, fearing he might change his mind, quickly accepted the footman's help and hurried into the waiting carriage.

Cae was soon out of the doors of the castle, but Niamh's husband had not entered the fortress that was their home.

She could see his eyes, watching Cae as she stepped into the carriage with a bright smile on her face, and a thank you to the footman. As the door closed, Niamh held her breath at his narrowed eyes, praying he didn't forbid her to go after all.

As they started off, the carriage rattled over the cobblestones, and Niamh, despite the distance, could swear she felt the intensity of her husband's stare. The weight of it was heavier than the carriage itself.

A silent promise of retribution hung in the air above Niamh for this small taste of freedom.

Chapter 4

Niamh followed Cae through the marketplace, staring at Cae's blond hair braided back into a crown. Cae's hands relaxed at her sides and, oh, how Niamh wished she could hold Cae's hand in public. To let the world know of their love.

But there were too many people there who knew she was the Lady of Waterford, so anything she did in the market would get back to her husband.

Which is why Niamh was terrified of going to a female apothecary. The hushed whispers among the elite labeled such women as witches, their eyes gleaming with suspicion and fear as they spoke the damning words in hushed tones.

If Lord Gwyer found out about her visiting...

"Oh, dear! My purse must have fallen off and I have no coin!" With an exaggerated flourish, Cae turned toward the guard her husband had assigned to escort them both into town, holding the broken purse string at her waist.

The female servant that was with them was younger, but Babette had promised Niamh that they could trust her.

Niamh hoped that was true.

"Lady Agnew—"

"Can you not find my purse? Oh, I would hate for the Lord to find out." Cae offered the guard a sad, tight-lipped smile, her hands clasped against her chest.

A stark pallor washed over the guard's face at the sound of Lord Agnew's name, his knuckles whitening as he clenched his fists at his sides. No one dared incur Lord Agnew's wrath; doing so invariably meant facing the even more formidable displeasure of Lord Gwyer. And to find out it was a man in his employ as a retainer, wearing the Waterford livery, well, that was even worse.

Looking toward the female servant, he nodded. "Stay here. I will look and find your purse." Turning to walk away, he looked back, hesitation clear in his pinched expression. "Do not move. The morning crowd was bustling and noisy. Street vendors, hurried footsteps, and a blacksmith's clangor almost drowned out his command.

As soon as he was out of sight, Niamh and Cae took off, the servant with them saying nothing, but following.

"She is amazing at herbal remedies for most everything that can ail a person, and ... more." Cae offered Niamh a tight, nervous smile, a stark contrast to her usual radiant grin. No, Cae knew what this meant for Niamh, for them both.

Any plan they had to run away would be gone, and that was tantamount to death in Niamh's opinion. She couldn't endure the suffocating control of Lord Gwyer, and the thought of a future without Cae was unbearable.

"However," Cae whispered as she moved in closer to Niamh, "it would be best if you let me lead. What we're asking for isn't something women like us are permitted to do, not without risking severe consequences."

The decision of when and how to have children was out of a woman's hands, a reality imposed upon them by their new faith. Their very fate lay in the hands of the men in their lives.

Niamh dreamed of a day when she could claim ownership of her body, and damn anyone who dared to challenge her, or any woman, to the depths of hell.

Cae slowed as they came upon a small shop at the end of an alleyway on the very edge of the market. The stone building full of shops ended abruptly after the heavy wooden door, marking where the dark forest met the cobbled market streets.

The shop door looked identical to the others on the street; worn wood, a tarnished brass knob—yet a deep sense of foreboding settled in Niamh's stomach, hinting at something significant behind it.

"M' Lady," the servant girl warned, "I do na think I can follow in good conscience."

Cae stopped, her gaze lingering on Niamh's face, the weight of the decision heavy in the air, but Cae was allowing her to choose their next step. Turning to the younger woman, Niamh bent a little, so they were at eye level.

"I understand. If you are unsure, stay out here and I shall make haste, but no one must know I was here. Do you understand?"

With a hesitant nod, the girl turned away, and Niamh followed Cae into the small apothecary shop. The scent of herbs and strange potions filling her nostrils as her heartbeat thrummed like a hummingbird's wings and her throat tightened with anxiety.

A sweet, melodic tinkle of silver chimes greeted them as they stepped into an open room filled with vibrant, green leaves of every shade imaginable. The earthy scent of petrichor hung heavily in the air, and a bird's harsh squawk pierced the silence, making Niamh gasp, her hand flying to her chest.

'Ello!" An older woman emerged from a dimly lit back room, her presence filling the space with the scent of wood smoke and damp earth. She moved behind a worn wooden counter, her deep, knowing eyes watching them intently as her gnarled fingers, surprisingly nimble, wove a vine basket.

With a sudden flutter of wings, the bird that had startled Niamh settled onto the older woman's shoulder, its tiny claws gently gripping the fabric as the woman moved.

The older woman placed the branch down before wiping her hands off on her apron, shuffling to get a better look at her new customers.

"Is that you, my darling Cae?" croaked the woman, her voice trembling like the leaves in the fall breeze, mirroring her frail body.

"It is, and I've finally brought the friend I've told you all about."

The older woman offered a smile, revealing a few broken teeth, yet her eyes crinkled warmly, conveying a genuine friendliness that Niamh found comforting.

"Ah, the lovely Niamh held back by a useless cock of a husband."

Niamh's eyebrows shot up in surprise, her hand flying to her mouth to stifle a gasp that escaped despite her best efforts; Cae just waved off the words dismissively. "There are no secrets here."

The older woman chortled. "What can I do for you?"

"Niamh received news that her husband wants an heir."

"Oh, he informed her she would be pregnant and would like it, eh?" The woman's voice spit out the last words. Turning, she grumbled as she worked on something Niamh couldn't quite see.

"...just supposed to be quiet and take it... to hell with the lot of them..."

Niamh smiled, a strange mix of amusement and understanding, at the older woman's enraged murmurs, words that echoed the fury Niamh herself often felt, a dark fire hidden deep inside.

She stepped toward the shelves, noticing the way the vines snaked down them. Niamh studied the books and jars of plants, noting the texture of the aged leather and the unique smells of each plant.

Flipping through the worn tomes, their aged leather soft beneath her fingertips, she felt the woman's love for the knowledge they held. Each page, delicately turned and lovingly handled, showed clear signs of being cherished.

Soon, the older woman's grumbling faded into a gentle hum, and the vines swayed towards the woman; the air felt charged with a strange energy.

Niamh almost dropped the book, its weight suddenly heavy in her trembling hands. She tried to reason why the vines, thick and strangely alive, would move in such an unnatural way. Carefully placing the book back, she slowly turned, watching the sunlight filter through the leaves as the vines gently touched the woman's arm.

"She will make sure you are just fine." Cae's hand, warm and reassuring, enveloped Niamh's, but Niamh, her heart pounding, intertwined their fingers. It was dangerous to act on such an impulse with a stranger nearby, but Niamh needed her lover's reassuring touch.

"Perhaps after this, we could take a ride out—"

"Here we go!" With a sharp turn, the older woman interrupted Cae, and Niamh quickly dropped Cae's hand, stepping back as the woman placed a small, mysterious-looking opaque vial on the counter. Carefully, Niamh reached out, her fingers brushing against the cool glass, and took the stoppered bottle, unplugging it to inhale the potent aroma.

Niamh barely stifled a gag but placed the stopper back into the vial. Giving a small, hesitant smile, she placed the vial back on the counter and pulled several coins from her purse.

The woman's hands were on Niamh's the moment she dropped the coins on the counter, the exact amount Cae had told her to bring. Niamh looked up to see the woman's eyes held a clarity that seemed at odds with her age.

"Take it when the sun sets and not a moment before." The woman held her hand tight until Niamh nodded, then released her.

"It tastes wretched." Cae winked at Niamh before turning to the older woman. "Thank you." Cae took the woman's gnarled hands and gave her a nod of her head in respect.

With her own thanks, Niamh pocketed the vial and waved goodbye to the older woman as Cae took her elbow and led her from the apothecary.

Niamh felt a sharp tugging sensation in her chest, like a trapped bird struggling for flight, before the pressure released as they stepped over the threshold of the shop. They stopped before the servant girl, her eyebrows high in surprise.

"Was she not in?"

Niamh started to say something, to ask how long she thought they had been there, but Cae waved her off. "Closed for the day. Nothing to fuss over." Weaving her arm through Niamh's, Cae pulled her out of the alleyway just as the retainer returned, a small purse in his hand.

Sensing eyes on them, Niamh turned to look back at the alleyway, but Cae kept tugging her along. Yet, the feeling of being watched only grew as Niamh went about the market.

Chapter 5

Returning home, Niamh felt her body momentarily freeze in fear as her husband's booming voice echoed throughout the fortress of Waterford Manor.

"What in the heavens..." Cae and Niamh looked at the footman, who shook his head, his eyes wide and fearful.

The sounds of her husband's slurred speech and angry shouts made Niamh hesitate; it was clearly another one of his drunken outbursts.

Despite this, his primal, unrestrained fury had never been unleashed so publicly since he always confined it to behind closed doors. That he was in such a terrifying rage implied he was beyond reason, and one could almost smell the volatile energy. Had something terrible happened in her absence?

Niamh entered the room, her jaw set, shoulders squared, as the staff whispered around her husband and Cae's. All of them looked stiff as statues, their muscles tense, a palpable pressure hanging in the air like a brewing storm.

The malice in her husband's red-veined eyes terrified her, but the look of narrowed suspicion from Cae's husband had the hair on the back of her neck stand on end.

"Lord Agnew has come at my request, wife," Niamh's husband announced. His voice was tight with barely controlled rage, his eyes darting between her and Cae, a simmering fury evident in their depths.

"Oh?" Niamh clasped her hands, her knuckles white, and fought to keep her trembling under control.

Her husband's booming laugh echoed as he pulled out a familiar piece of parchment, the brittle edges crinkling as he waved it wildly. One that Niamh had forgotten about, a detail lost in the quiet chaos of Babette already being in her room and her husband's imminent arrival.

A chill ran down Niamh's spine, mirroring Cae's sudden stillness as their eyes locked, but Cae swiftly masked her fear with a neutral facade.

"Come now, Lord Gwyer—" But before Cae could utter an excuse, Niamh's husband, with predatory grace, was closing in.

"Oh, you think to speak to me when you lay with my wife under my nose?" he seethed.

Cae's husband stepped between Cae and Lord Gwyer, his hands up. "Now, this could have been anything. Perhaps we are taking it out of context. The ladies have a strong friendship."

"Oh?" Lord Gwyer let out a low growl, snatching the paper and unfolding it with a sharp crackle. "The softest touch of your hand on my thigh—"

With a sudden burst of panic, Niamh lunged across the room, the parchment tearing slightly as she wrenched it from her husband's hand.

It took only a fraction of a second before his hand, which had just held the paper, was cinching around her throat like a noose, cutting off her breath.

"A wanton woman has no place in this world. Especially one who lays with her own," he snarled.

Lord Agnew's commanding order to halt cut the sound of Cae's approach short. "It is his place as her husband to discipline her."

Niamh's face burned with anger; oh, how she wished she could rip the tongue out of his mouth and silence him forever. To make every single bastard in the room pay until they begged for mercy.

"You will do as I bid. No longer will you have free rein to make a fool of me." With a harsh last squeeze around her throat, he shoved her away, the sudden release causing a racking cough. He then commanded Babette, who had been watching from the doorway, to take her to her room and lock the door behind her.

Tears welled in Cae's eyes, but Niamh stood firm, refusing to retreat like a whipped dog.

As much as both her heart and body hurt, she held her head high and walked out of the room of her own accord, where both her tormentor and her lover stood watching.

Not for the first time did Niamh wish she had the magic of the old gods so she could hex the man her father had sold her off to.

Chapter 6

When Niamh refused to come down for dinner, she was thankful her husband did not come to her room to demand her attendance. The thought of him witnessing her tears, of seeing her vulnerability and reveling in her pain, was unbearable.

Grief-stricken, she sought solace in the darkness of her room. Niamh clutched her mother's soft, wool blanket, its familiar scent a small comfort amidst the overwhelming sorrow that burrowed deep into her soul.

A hard knock on her door had her opening her swollen eyes from the sleep she'd slid into when she'd exhausted herself from crying.

The continued pounding on the door finally roused Niamh; she shivered, pulling her blanket tighter as she stumbled towards it, the dull ache behind her eyes intensifying with each thud.

Her heart pounded a frantic rhythm against her ribs as she turned the heavy, cold iron doorknob. Her breath caught in her throat at the sight of her father's intense, black eyes staring at her from across the threshold.

Stepping toward her, her father grabbed her elbow, his rough fingers digging into her skin as she tried to pull away, the force of his grasp making her wince.

"If it's true, you'd be lucky to breathe another day in this world. Pray your husband is merciful, because I wouldn't be." The rancid smell of his tobacco-stained breath washed over her as he snarled the vicious threat.

As her husband's heavy footsteps sounded, her father let her go. He then bowed to Lord Gwyer, showering him with the same empty compliments he always offered when kissing his boot.

Numb, she strode into the hallway, eyes downcast, to conclude the matter of her fate.

"I hope you will forgive my daughter for her trespass this time, my Lord. She is weak willed, like her mother."

Oh, Niamh wanted to snap the man's fingers one by one for speaking of her mother in such a way, but she looked down instead, biting into her lip until she tasted copper.

"I do believe you've said enough. I will handle my own wife." Her husband's unwavering gaze burned into her, but Niamh's eyes darted away, unable to bear the intensity of his stare. She felt childish in doing so, but it was like looking into the very eyes of death itself. "Return to your room, wife, and wait for me while I have your father taken care of."

With a hesitant step back, she started towards her room, the weight of her father's question—"Do you plan to keep her? There's no place for her in my home any longer"—hung heavily in the air.

Deciding she did not want to hear the answer, Niamh went to the window overlooking the quiet front gardens and waited. Her breath misted on the glass as her father appeared on the lawn, her husband remaining by the door.

Looking up at her, her father's haggard face met her gaze. His face contorted into a mask of disgust, his nostrils flaring as he turned to leave.

A timid knock, too gentle to be her husband's, preceded the opening of the door, revealing two maids, neither of whom was Babette. Their pity was a tangible thing as they readied her for bed, and she couldn't meet their eyes, instead she focused on the familiar worn surface of the dressing table. Her eyes watered and the world blurred around her as they silently finished their tasks and left the room as quietly as they entered.

Though her husband wouldn't evict her, he'd make her life an absolute misery with constant, petty cruelties. Even more so than he already did.

Her gaze fell upon the ornate mahogany drawer containing the small glass vial she'd obtained. With steady steps, she opened the drawer. Her fingers brushed against the cool, smooth wood as she reached for the elixir, and held it up to the soft light filtering through the window. Pulling the stopper from the opaque glass, she took a ragged breath of courage and tipped the vial back against her lips.

Hearing the footfalls of her husband, she threw the vial back in the drawer of her vanity, grimacing as she swallowed down the gritty substance. Turning to the door just as it swung inward with a loud creak, she saw her husband silhouetted in the doorway, his dark coat seeming to swallow the dim light. He nodded curtly to his men outside the room, their faces impassive, their eyes like chips of flint. She had a feeling they were chosen to shadow her every step going forward since any semblance of freedom was now lost to her forever.

"Wife." The harsh, gravelly tone of his voice was jarring, a discordant sound that grated against her sensitive nerves. "I am a merciful man." He sat in a chair near her hearth, untying his boots. "That I would allow you to continue under my roof after such horrific discretions, ones which would have the devil at my door, makes me wonder if I am mad." She remained silent, her eyes fixed on him as he slowly removed his boots before shedding his outer clothes. The rustle of linen was a quiet counterpoint to the rising tension until he stood before her in only his shirt and trousers. "But you are beautiful, and so ultimately, how can I punish you for the curse of your beauty calling to others?"

He gently grazed his knuckle across her cheek before he moved his hand into her hair, his fingers tangling through the dark, unbound tresses as he yanked her head back. "But," he whispered, his breath warm against her ear, "you no longer will be allowed to err in such ways going forward. I will dictate every decision you make. Everywhere you go, I will be there. Never again will I leave you to your own devices since you are far too weak a woman to know that what I say is law."

And Niamh knew he meant every word. He would kill her should she try to have an ounce of independent thought.

With a slow, deliberate movement, he reached for the edges of her robe, carefully pushing it down her arms so that it fell in a soft heap at her feet. His eyes raked over her, lingering on every inch, making her skin crawl with a sense of violation and shame.

Closing her eyes, she bit into her lip to hold the tears at bay. Niamh knew that what she had thought of as a prison before was nothing compared to the hell it would become.

Chapter 7

Niamh didn't rise the next day until the maid knocked on the door before letting herself in.

Her eyes, red and swollen from crying, mirrored Niamh's, but Niamh understood the source of her tears, and not the maid's.

Sitting up in her bed, the maid ignored her for the most part, sniffling as she worked to stoke the fire again and pick out Niamh's dress for the day.

"What has happened?" Niamh asked, her throat dry and raw, a scratchy rasp in her voice. Pushing back the covers, Niamh stood when the maid said nothing. "I demand to know why you are crying."

The maid wouldn't meet her gaze, her head shaking, before a deluge of tears poured down her face, accompanied by a choked sob. The woman frantically wiped at her cheeks, leaving streaks of wetness across her skin.

"I am out of work, miss. It's not the worst thing to happen, but my ma, she—" a bang on the door had the maid squeaking and jumping in fright, hurrying away from Niamh. "I must ready you before I leave."

Looking from the door to the maid, Niamh nodded, not wanting to make more trouble for the girl.

The maid's quiet sobs and the hushed rustle of fabric were a backdrop to the storm of theories brewing in Niamh's mind. Each idea was a desperate attempt to make sense of the fact the maid was out of work.

The Lord of the house must have taken his wrath out on the servants once he finished with Niamh. It was the only thing that made sense, but to let them go? How many were being displaced?

"All done, miss. Please..." the young girl's eyes darted to the door, before she lowered her voice. "Please don't make it worse for the ones who have to stay. They're only doing what they're told and they need the work just as bad."

Without waiting for an answer, the maid flew from the room, her footsteps echoing on the polished floor in her escape.

Niamh took in the same two men from the night before, still standing guard in the hallway. A new face moved into the room, holding the door with a stone-faced expression as he waited for her to leave. They looked everywhere but at her, and she knew they had orders to drag her out if she didn't comply.

It wouldn't have been the first time, but this felt all too much like she was being walked to her execution.

Her thoughts moved to the staff as she left the room, keeping her distance from the men as she walked down the stairs to see what was happening.

As she descended the creaking wooden stairs, the hushed goodbyes and the rustle of packed belongings from the Waterford Castle staff filled the air, a poignant symphony of farewells.

The now jobless group consisted solely of women, and Niamh knew then it was because of her they were now unemployed.

"What has happened?" She froze midway down the stairs.

"Please, continue down, my lady," one man from behind her whispered, the plea in his voice evident.

"The master is having all women in the home removed." Another of the men spoke up.

With a rising fury, Niamh snatched up her skirts and stormed down the remaining stairs, the noise of the crowd a dull roar as her eyes hunted for Babette. Not finding her closest friend in the household, she went hunting for her husband.

He sat at the breakfast table, ignoring the women at the door with their packed bags while guards searched their belongings as if they were criminals.

"You fired all the women?" Niamh asked, trying not to scream the words at him and make it all worse.

"I cannot trust you to keep your lustful demons at bay, and so I am helping. Now, sit and eat. You could be carrying my heir, and you must care for that child, since it is all that guarantees I will keep you alive and well."

A howl of anger met them, a scuffle in the front gardens breaking Niamh's glare on her husband.

"What is going on?" she stepped toward the window, but her husband was quick enough to stop her, his hand tight on her shoulder.

"I was merciful, but not all who dared to defy me were so lucky."

A man, one Niamh recognized as the gardener, his clothes muddied and torn, scrambled into the parlor, his eyes wild and bloodshot from a sleepless night.

His fury exploded in a guttural yell, "You bastard!", the words thick with pain, his usually pristine appearance now reflecting his inner turmoil. Not only was he the gardener, but he was Babette's suitor, one that Babette had planned to marry soon.

The three men who had brought her downstairs grappled with Babette's intended. "Stop that!" Niamh ordered before she spun to face her husband.

He had slid back into his seat as he took a bite of his eggs, unaffected, as if the scene playing out was all very normal.

"I could not trust her because she allowed an affair to continue in my home, right under my nose."

Stepping toward him, Niamh swore under her breath. "You fired Babette?"

He smiled as he finished a bite of toast. "No."

Fear flooded Niamh's veins. She was intelligent enough to understand Babette's fate in what was left unsaid.

"You're more demon than man." Niamh's voice was barely a whisper, strained and tight as she forced the words out.

With a furious shove from the table, her husband sent his chair skidding back, the sudden noise stark against the rising tension. He stalked toward her, a predator's gleam in his eyes, his every step heavy with menace, and she couldn't shake the chilling question of whether he'd done it himself or hired someone.

A cruel smile twisted his lips as he said, "I am the Lord of this estate. To every soul on this very land, from the lowest stable boy to the highest chef, I am their God!" Niamh felt the corner of the room at her back, with nowhere to escape, his body caging her in, and his breath hot on her face. "As I am your God and you will obey me unless you plan to join Babette."

His eyes locked on hers until he found what he wanted, and only then did he nod and return to the table.

"Let her finish her tantrum while you see the gardener out. I do not want to hear his pathetic whimpering as well."

As the men roughly led Babette's intended away, Niamh felt a fiery rage burn in her chest, constricting her breath. The grief, a searing fire in her soul, still burned, defying her husband's attempts to extinguish it with his controlling words and orders.

Niamh pushed away from the wall, her body heaving with barely contained rage, and stared at her tormentor, who calmly continued his breakfast, seemingly oblivious to the devastation he'd wrought.

"You are no god," she growled, her voice low and dangerous. Walking toward the table, her hand moved over the silver until the handle of a knife was in her white knuckled grip. Her husband only responded with a chuff of laughter.

"What do you plan to do with that, wife? If you kill me, will the townspeople not chase you out to where you would live and die a pauper?"

With a fierce grip on the handle, she charged, her blade tearing into his chest, a fraction of an inch from his dark, unfeeling heart.

Niamh ripped it out; his howl of pain was deafening as her own battle cry filled the air. She would force the dark, demonic blood from his heart, each drop a testament to her rage and a sickening reminder of his evil.

The sound of his hand striking her face was deafening, a sharp sting that brought tears to her eyes. His scream was a horrifying blend of rage and hatred. But despite that, she refused to yield. She needed his blood on her hands, to feel his heart beat its last and squeeze the life out of it before she burned it in a pit. A promise to the world he would never come back.

Shoving him with all her might, she swung the knife to stab him again, the sounds of panicked footsteps and shouts echoing as people burst into the room. Her husband used her own momentum to swiftly bring her back against him, his hands grabbing her head and squeezing as he uttered, "See you in hell, Niamh."

And with a snap, Niamh lost the battle but finally found her freedom from the man she called her husband.

Chapter 8

Niamh gasped awake, her mouth dry and cracked, her tongue thick and heavy, a gritty, sandy coating clinging to her throat. A thirst unlike any she'd ever experienced consumed her, her stomach twisting with a gnawing emptiness.

Pure darkness surrounded her. Panic set in as she thrashed, her hands hitting a rough wall mere inches from her face, showering her with dirt. Feeling around, she finally understood the gravity of the situation. She was in a coffin.

Niamh had died at her husband's hands ... or so she thought.

A rhythmic sound above her had her hoping that meant it was the way up. As she struck the weathered wood, a cascade of dirt and crumbling fragments rained down. The sheer panic of being buried alive, the smell of damp soil filling her nostrils, fueled her frantic efforts to escape. The wood groaned, unyielding. Terror seized her, overriding logic, as she hammered at the wooden coffin of her grave, splintering it with each blow.

With a crash, a hole appeared in the wood, and the rush of soil and earth sent a wave of suffocating horror through her.

Clawing at the dirt, she pulled herself upward, the gritty soil filling her mouth and ears as she struggled.

A wave of nausea washed over her as the surrounding soil trembled. The gritty texture of the earth scratching against her skin as she ascended, her body frozen in shock as the earth moved her. When she broke through the surface, firm hands grasped hers and pulled her up.

Overwhelmed with relief, she sank to her knees beside her grave, the cold ground seeping into her clothes. Tremors racked her body, each cough bringing up more dirt and a burning pain in her throat as she curled into herself.

Her gritty eyes opened to reveal two strangers bathed in the silvery light of the full moon: a man and a woman, their voices a low murmur of the old tongue. Niamh recalled her mother's lessons. The ancient words of the gods and the reverence for the children of Danu before the church's arrival shattered their world, silencing the ancient songs and rituals.

The male approached her, raising his hands in a gesture of peace as he kneeled, his golden eyes intense.

His skin was luminescent in the moonlight, reminding her of an ethereal creature. A fae perhaps, but his long hair was down, and so she could not see his ears. "It seems to have worked," he said in a deep, resonant voice.

"Of course it did!" The woman giggled, her hands moving out to her sides, and the earth moved with her gesture, lifting Niamh into a sitting position.

A strong sense of déjà vu washed over her, but she couldn't place where she knew the woman from.

"Oh!" The woman smiled. "You do not recognize me!"

Her form shifted, growing old and gnarled as she became the apothecary woman from the market. The scent of herbs clinging to her, before transforming back into the striking beauty with leaves woven through her long, blonde hair. She watched Niamh with golden eyes, and like the male, her alabaster skin glowed with an inner light. Both of them wore dark green cloaks, their hoods back, but the female's cloak was open. Her dress was the green of fresh spring grass and a torc of gold around her neck.

"Who are you?" A strangled gasp escaped Niamh's lips as she battled the overwhelming instinct to run, her limbs leaden and unresponsive in the grip of the powerful beings before her. "What did you do to me?"

With a serene smile, the woman said, "Children of Danu, my sweet Niamh," her voice soft as a summer breeze. "As for what I did, I gave you a potion to make you immortal since you have been chosen to help us. I knew the moment I saw your face that you were the one from the vision our sister told us of."

They were a god and a goddess, standing in a graveyard as if Niamh was someone of vast importance.

"You're sure she is the one from the vision?" the male asked, his hand finding Niamh's shoulder, his touch grounding her, the fear receding as strength flowed into her limbs.

"Well, of course she is! When has the Morrigan ever been mistaken before?" the woman replied, and the male gave Niamh a wink before stepping back to give her space.

"The... the Morrigan?" Niamh gasped, her eyes darting between the two figures. A whirlwind of confusion and fear swirled in her mind as she wondered how the war goddess factored into this strange situation. Suddenly, Niamh remembered the goddess also helped people to cross to the Otherworld. "Did I not earn my death? Am I trapped here?"

Despite the god's calming power, a visible tremor ran through her, her body shaking violently. The thought of being stuck in between, not alive and not dead...

"You earned more than that, but I am not the one who can tell you all. I was only to help make everything come to fruition. When she is ready to speak with you, she will." With a graceful movement, the woman floated forward, her cloak swirling slightly as she gently took Niamh's hands, pulling her to her feet. A delightful warmth, like a sunbeam on a winter's day, spread through Niamh's body. She knew it was the woman's power, and she would feel cold and dirty again as soon as the woman released her.

"You've earned your second chance at life, my dear, as well as your revenge."

Chapter 9

With the moon hanging high above, casting long shadows, Niamh stumbled along the cobbled streets, past dark, foreboding doorways. She made her way through Waterford, and only the power of the god and goddess from the grave-yard kept her thirst at bay.

Niamh silently walked the familiar roads, her tears cold against her dirt-stained cheeks, each sob echoing the quiet rhythm of her footsteps.

She stopped at a small, cluttered shop and gazed into the dusty window. Her reflection was a shock: pale, her eyes dark and sunken, less a survivor and more a wraith.

Yesterday, Niamh wore one of her beautiful dresses with her dark hair pinned up perfectly as she walked the very road she stood on.

Today, dark, clinging mud and sticky blood coated her body. In the light mist of rain and her tears, the kohl she used on her eyes melted and ran down her face, smudging into dark rivulets.

Niamh looked as if she was in the grasp of death, but the goddess had promised her she was still alive.

They gave her some details; she was alive, but not completely. She was a creature of the night now, the first of her kind. An unknown.

When the goddess tore open her wrist, Niamh descended upon the fresh blood with the hunger of a ravenous animal.

The experience disgusted Niamh afterward, but her thirst was too great to resist in the moment.

But that was how she would sustain herself now, and she wasn't sure if she would have preferred to be left to rot in the grave instead.

If she chose to, she could wait until the sun rose, the goddess had told her. Then, when day broke, she could let the rays of the sun give her true death.

The cold seeped into her bones, amplified by that chilling thought. Niamh rubbed her arms in a futile attempt to restore warmth to her freezing limbs.

Turning away from the horrifying image of herself, she continued through the city and down the farm roads, toward the castle where her father had sentenced her to death.

Her feet stopped when she crossed the path that would instead lead to her father's farm.

Anger and instinct drove her until she ran toward his home. With each strained breath, she forced the heavy gate open, the sound of its hinges groaning like a dying beast. Though her father now had livestock—scrawny, neglected creatures—from the coins he earned selling his daughter, his drinking and gambling squandered the remaining coin.

His home, the one her mother had taught her of the very gods that brought Niamh back, stood falling into disrepair.

The image only angered her further as she moved to the dark home, the moon casting ominous shadows, the home a mirror of Niamh. Dead inside, haunted, waiting for someone to burn it to ash.

Slamming open the door, and though the home was not much compared to the castle at Waterford, it was still a decent size and would have made a respectable home for a family.

Now, a pompous ass was running it into the ground.

A torch sputtered to life, casting dancing shadows as her father moved down the long hall, having undoubtedly heard the commotion.

He muttered, "Damn wind...," then stopped dead in his tracks upon seeing Niamh. "Sluagh!"

She threw back her head and laughed as the smell of urine filled the air.

"Hello, father. You believe in the old ways now?" Niamh walked closer to him. The stink of his fear made her canines elongate. "That I've come for your useless soul?"

"You are not Niamh! Your eyes..." As her father spoke, she could see the vein in her father's neck pulsing with oxygen-rich blood. "Whatever I've done, I am sorry!"

He scrambled back as she stalked toward him.

"Yes, father, what could you have possibly done? Perhaps it was when you left me with an abusive husband for the coin you gambled away. Or that you let mother die, penniless and destroyed while you met with working women and squandered what you took for my hand."

"I... I never meant—"

Niamh's rage exploded, cutting off his words as she launched herself across the room, a whirlwind of fury aimed at ending him and those who had wronged her. The air crackled with her furious anger. A low growl vibrating in her chest, her fangs sinking into his neck as she felt his last gasp, his body falling limp in her arms as she lost herself.

When the metallic tang of blood flooded her mouth, it tasted far sweeter than Niamh could have imagined.

Niamh arrived at Waterford Castle where the flickering torchlight of the night watch cast long shadows across the courtyard.

With a determined stride, she moved through the lush front lawn toward the castle, only to be stopped by the guards.

"Halt!" one yelled, and Niamh realized she didn't even know the guards' names. Nameless men her jealous husband had forbidden her to be sociable with until he finally understood it wasn't them that she desired.

Niamh pressed onward until the torchlight struck her face, silencing the guards with a sudden, sharp intake of breath.

"Lady Gwyer..." they spoke of her as if she were a ghost, and she supposed she was.

She was also dirty and covered in her father's blood.

A shared glance passed between the guards; fear etched on their faces, they instinctively parted to let her pass, their distress a silent barrier that kept them from hindering her further.

Opening the doors herself, she walked past a horrified and half-asleep footman. A faint, almost imperceptible smell of cooked game, perhaps pheasant, lingered in the air, a ghostly reminder of a recent feast.

Niamh climbed the stairs, the silence heavy, broken only by the rhythmic creak of the old wood under her feet. No one that was awake bothered to stop her.

As she neared her husband's room, she heard the muffled sounds of passion—moans, gasps, and the rhythmic thudding of bodies. The groans she knew all too well from nights of tolerating his touch. But the female voice was a recent addition.

His deep tenor voice yelled wicked curses and demands, followed by a feminine scream, as she threw open his door.

The dark held no secrets from Niamh's keen night vision. She could clearly see Lady Shaw's crimson cheeks and narrowed gaze as the woman tried to discern who dared interrupt them. The air still thick with the scent of their passion and the muffled sounds of her husband's struggle to make himself decent.

"Funny, Lady Shaw, you seem to have found yourself on the end of the wrong cock." Her eyes settled on Lord Gwyer, his expression unreadable, as Lady Shaw gasped at the sound of Niamh's voice.

"Hello, darling. It seems I have returned from the grave."

Chapter 10

"Niamh!" he shouted, the confusion and frustration in his voice palpable as he scrambled for his robe, which lay crumpled on the chair next to the bed.

"Oh, why bother, darling? I've seen the shriveled bit you were just mounting Lady Shaw with. Tell me, Lady Shaw, were your screams of passion real or simply a way to assuage his ego? Maybe that's why we never worked. I had to feel something for it to make me react."

Lady Shaw's body trembled violently; her eyes were wide, and her mouth hung open in shock, a silent scream trapped in her throat.

"Niamh!" Her husband was moving around the bed, his face redder than she'd ever seen, but she felt no fear. No, she had the upper hand this time.

"I suppose she was helping you through the grieving process," Niamh smiled sardonically, and Lord Gwyer hesitated, a tremor in his hands noticeable before he stood and straightened his shoulders.

"A mistake has been made. I thought you were dead, but here you are, in the flesh. All is well once again."

With a questioning tilt of her head, the silence amplified the tension between Niamh and her husband. Niamh could hear his heart pick up its beat the longer she stared at him, and she could almost smell the adrenaline flooding his veins.

"Well, you didn't bother with a wake, did you? Found that you couldn't get me beneath the dirt fast enough, could you, darling?"

Her eyes followed her husband's careful movements as he lit a candle. The soft glow illuminating the lines etched on his face, his eyes gleaming like embers in the warm firelight. With the new light, the smell of his fear subsided as he took her in, seeing she still was Niamh, if a bit more worn. She supposed she looked harmless enough; no sharp claws or teeth were visible, at least not yet.

"Well, you found your way out just fine. Witchcraft, perhaps, *darling?*" he mocked as she stepped further into the light. His taunting words fueled her rage, a fire that burned brighter even in death.

She would not yield.

"I would sew your lips shut had I the needle and thread to do so," she whispered before raising her voice and mimicking him. "Niamh! Niamh, you will do as I say! Niamh, I don't like your tone! Niamh, I am a *god!*" As she strolled toward her husband, the candlelight flickered, revealing the tremor of his shaking hands.

"I've seen gods, and you are *nothing* compared to them," she said as she stepped up against him, their chests touching, a smirk playing on her lips. "And no, darling, not witchcraft, but the will of the actual gods themselves."

Grabbing him by the throat, Lady Shaw's piercing scream, a sound like tearing silk, brought the guards thundering up the stairs. Niamh's nails grew longer, piercing through the skin of his neck.

Lady Shaw scrambled from the bed, silk sheets pooling around her as she slipped, her naked form stumbling as the door slammed open, revealing guards and a shocked Lord Shaw.

"Mary..." The profound sadness etched on Lord Shaw's features nearly pierced Nimah's icy composure, sparking a moment of unexpected empathy. He was older, but still a distinguished gentleman, and obviously had not been a party to his wife's plans to seduce the Lord of Waterford.

Lady Shaw hastily pulled a sheet around herself, tears silently tracing paths down her face. "I am so sorry, Thomas. I should have said no..."

"Oh, Mary didn't even have to say no. For months she has worked herself silly to get into my bed, and I relented." Lord Gwyer looked at Niamh. "A contingency plan in case you failed to produce an heir for me."

He'd imprisoned her, exiled her lover because of her actions, and continued his affair with another woman as if that wasn't the height of hypocrisy.

Men had all the power, but not anymore.

"I bet Cae would have enjoyed me too had she not been too dumb to fall into your arms."

With a guttural scream that tore through the silence, Niamh's reason snapped. A frenzied lunge ended with her fangs tearing into her husband's throat; the sounds of ripping flesh and the hot rush of blood were overwhelming. His scream, a high-pitched, desperate sound, devolved into a gurgling gasp as she drained the life from him. The full impact of the brutal decapitation—the rip, the twist—didn't hit her until she lifted his head, the reality of her actions still dawning.

The screams were deafening, the blood a horrifying crimson tide coating her throat and running down her face, overwhelming her senses and driving her mind to the brink of madness.

Tossing Lord Gwyer's head aside, she licked her fingers clean before a sound caught her attention. A sob.

Niamh stalked towards the sound; the air thick with anticipation. The frantic beat of Lady Shaw's heart grew louder until Niamh felt it beneath her teeth, the metallic tang of blood filling her senses as she drank.

Not hunger, but a white-hot fury, sharp as shattered glass, and the agonizing sting of painful memories drove her on.

In a frenzy of violence, she carved a path through the room as the men in her husband's employ rushed to attack her. Her actions were driven by primal instinct and the sounds of her victims' gasps.

Did they not all fail to intervene, leaving her to scream endlessly while they stood by, ignoring her pleas as her husband did as he pleased? Leaving her to be battered and beaten while they went about their day.

They may not have hurt her themselves, but they were just as guilty.

Niamh came back to herself when she stepped out of the room, Lord Shaw shivering outside the door, but Niamh left him alone. He'd done nothing to earn her ire and was as much a victim as she was.

Stepping past him, her feet hit the top of the stairs with a heavy thud. The sickening slosh of blood inside her a grim counterpoint to the overpowering smell of decaying flesh and urine that filled her former home, the sounds and smells a horrifying symphony in her psyche.

Hitting the bottom step, something fell against the floor, bringing her head up, her nose scenting prey.

The hushed whispers and fearful glances of the servants huddled in the dimly lit corner of the sitting room met Niamh. Clenching her bloodied fists, the metallic tang of blood filling her nostrils, she pulled herself back from the precipice of her blood lust. She would leave them to live another day and unwittingly start the legend of the Dearg Due.

Blood, still wet and glistening, stained Niamh's clothes as she left Waterford Castle for the last time.

Chapter 11

Niamh raced towards the Agnew estate, the darkness barely illuminated by the faintest hint of dawn, her breath misting in the frigid air as she pushed herself onward.

She was strong enough now that she and Cae could run away together and start a new life somewhere else. No one could stop them now.

As she ran, Niamh slowed upon entering the grounds of the estate. The darkened house was unnervingly still. The maids should have lit the torches as they tended the fires and readied the home for the Lord and Lady to wake.

Maybe ... Maybe Cae and her husband ran away to avoid her husband's wrath. It meant that Niamh would have to look for her, but that Cae was alive and well was all she truly cared about.

A palpable sense of dread overwhelmed her as she walked into the large, silent home, where she found every mirror covered with dark cloth. Dust motes danced in the sunbeams slanting through the windows of the empty house, illuminating the furniture covered in protective sheets.

A bitter wave of grief washed over Niamh as the grim reality settled in her stomach—Cae was lost to her forever.

She felt every ounce of her resolve to live die out as a crushing weight settled on her chest, a physical manifestation of her overwhelming sorrow. A raw, desperate howl escaped her lips, amplifying the anguish that clawed at her heart.

Knowing the family graveyard was close, Niamh stumbled outside where the scent of freshly turned earth filled the air from two new graves; Niamh's gaze, however, remained fixed on a single one.

Beside her lover's grave, shrouded in an ethereal mist, stood the goddess who played at being an apothecary and the very architect of Niamh's despair.

"You let her die!" Niamh yelled, her knees buckling, but she forced herself to the grave, collapsing onto the cold, damp earth. Cae's grave dirt mingled with the soil still under Niamh's fingernails from digging herself out of her own grave.

To her surprise, the goddess sat down too. "I did not intend for her to lose her life. She was such a bright soul; I was sure she had more time."

Sniffling, Niamh fought to maintain composure.

"He killed them..." Even though not phrased as a question, the goddess still responded.

"Soon after your funeral, he sent word to Cae that you had died." The goddess laid her hand on the soil. "It was too much for her and she chose her end instead of letting your husband take that choice from her. Her husband followed." The goddess looked to Cae's home, sympathy in her eyes.

"He as good as killed her," Niamh whispered. "I did not have to read the letter he would have sent her to know it was a hateful concoction of taunts and wicked words, each syllable a cruel blow."

"I will not argue that both his words and actions led to this outcome."

Niamh repeated, "He killed her," as she laid her head onto the rain-soaked soil of the grave.

The act of revenge left her with an icy emptiness, a hollowness that echoed the chill in the air. What was the point of it all if she couldn't share her freedom with the one person she loved most?

In the end, her revenge had only taken what was left of her humanity, as did the death of the woman she loved.

"I swear, I shall never let another man treat me as they treated us," Niamh whispered, ignoring the goddess who watched with sad eyes. "I wish I could have saved you, but I will join you soon enough."

The sun would rise, and Niamh would let it take her. The only way she could know true death, she had been told.

"You will. It won't be in the way you think, but you will." The goddess held out her hand, something in her palm. "I have no answers. Those belong to my sister, but I was tasked with making you this."

The goddess uncurled her hand, revealing a blood-red stone necklace that shimmered with an inner light before she closed her fingers again, leaving it dangling alluringly before Niamh.

"It is of your love, and so with it, you will be bound to her through all your lives."

Niamh pulled the stone closer, its warmth spreading from her fingertips through the rest of her body, and she could feel life thrumming from within the stone. How the goddess got the essence of Cae in the stone, Niamh didn't know.

Closing her eyes, Niamh curled onto her side, the damp mist clinging to her skin as silent tears streamed down her face. The goddess waited for a time with her, running her fingers over Niamh's hair before she slowly disappeared.

The rhythmic thud of hoofbeats on the packed earth leading to the graveyard shattered her morose thoughts. Light shone from the corner of her eye, and initially mistaking it for the sun, she quickly realized the light was actually from a group of men carrying torches, trespassing on Cae's property.

"The demon is here!" One yelled, and Niamh knew she had a decision to make. She could let these men have her, torture her, and do who knew what else, or she could live another day. Niamh could escape and take the time to decide on her own fate instead of once again letting men decide it for her.

With a kiss to the soil, Niamh stood.

A low, raspy feminine voice spoke up behind her. "I'd suggest you find somewhere dark and quiet." Niamh spun, almost tripping over her skirts, startled by the unexpected presence of a very different goddess.

With her black hair in tight braids, pointed ears, black sclera, red irises, and pale skin adorned with blue war paint and intricate tattoos, she was a terrifying vision. The very image of the goddess of war, death, and witchcraft from her mother's tales.

Niamh was a tall woman, but this woman towered over her, her height surpassing that of most men. But Niamh imagined the goddess's aura, not her height, was powerful enough to halt even the most feral fighters in their tracks.

The Morrigan looked over Niamh's shoulder and nodded toward the crowd growing closer. "Time to make a choice. You can let them drag you through the streets until sunrise for both a painful and useless death, or you can be of help to the gods themselves."

Niamh shuddered, running her hands over her arms to both calm her nerves and fortify herself. Now that death was baring down on her, she knew she wasn't ready. She wanted to contemplate it, not to be forced into it.

Before thinking of the ramifications of her other choice, she nodded. "What do you need of me?

The goddess nodded to the bloodstone that hung at her throat. "You've had your revenge, but what I need from you will take a lifetime, maybe more than one. It is what the visions have shown me. In the end, should you help, you will find a peace you never knew was possible and have only dreamed of."

She could barely see beyond the harsh glare of the torches. Its light growing uncomfortably near as the death calls pierced the silence, drowned out only by the pounding of her heart. Niamh wanted to ask more questions but knew her time was running out.

"Will I be expected to bend a knee for men?"

The Morrigan smiled. "Never again."

Squaring her shoulders, Niamh nodded, a determined glint in her eyes.

"Then I am at your service, my goddess."

The moment she spoke, the world shimmered around Niamh. The colors muting as she phased into a world identical to her own but invisible to the approaching men with their pitchforks and torches. Their confused shouts echoing around her when she was no longer visible.

Turning to the goddess, the Morrigan laughed as she watched the men spinning and yelling before she returned her focus to Niamh. "You are in the veil between worlds, and here you are safe from the sun, but it will take much from you. Use it sparingly."

Ignoring the men, Niamh held the eyes of the deity. "What do you ask of me?"

"That the day we meet again, though you may not know me, you will care for my vessel until it is time for me to rise again. It will be long after this world falls to the chaos of the Fomori, when the earth shakes and rivers of lava flow. When we have lost the battle, but not the war."

"I won't know you, but I am supposed to protect you?" Niamh considered the request. The meager details offered felt insufficient, leaving her feeling uneasy and uncertain about such an agreement.

"You will know me because when you see me, the blood debt will be paid," The Morrigan nodded at the red stone Niamh wore around her throat. "That stone will be your guide in finding me again."

"Do you know when or where?"

The Morrigan looked away, her eyes focused on something in the distance before she spoke.

"At the gate to hell."

Chapter 12

ONE YEAR LATER

The most challenging aspect of the afterlife for Niamh was controlling her blood-lust.

The prick of a needle when someone was sewing, that small bead of blood, was enough to make her salivate and have to excuse herself. Niamh knew to stay when blood was drawn would mean she could lose herself to that primal side of her, and so far, no one had survived it.

Replaying her last meal in her mind, she was hit by a wave of guilt, noting its similarity to the uncontrollable anger of a drunkard. The moment her fangs bit into their flesh, she drowned in the memory of her husband's death where time ceased to exist, her mind locked in that moment of violence.

Once the blood ran dry, she was holding a corpse and evidence of her murderous mistake.

Niamh was always on the run because of it. Time and time again being driven out by torch-wielding villagers after they found several of the young men in their town dead and it highlighted the urgent need for self-control. However, she was the first and only Dearg Due, utterly alone, and therefore, no one taught her to control her thirst ... or her violence.

So, she hunted men who thought themselves above both the law and gods, committing terrible crimes with no punishment to be had. Niamh made herself justice to calm her own burdened soul, but not everyone felt that way, and so Niamh had nowhere to call home.

And maybe she never would.

Growling, she threw her knitting needles across the rented room she'd found refuge at in a small town far, far from the last village to run her out. A farmer and his wife were lovely enough to let a bedraggled lady stay with them. She would not return their kindness by inadvertently sipping them dry in her attempts to learn how not to kill her dinner.

She could hear the farmer moving about with the last of his daily chores, and knew the night was upon them. The thick curtains hadn't been enough, so Niamh had thrown a blanket up, too. Thankfully the farmer and his wife were not the busybodies like some others she'd rented space from along the way in her travels.

It had been a year since she'd died. Having explored the rolling green hills and rugged coastlines of Ireland, she felt it was time to leave the island.

She neared the coast, aware of the dubious characters at the docks who, for the right price, would assist her in escaping without question.

Niamh knew that soon enough the towns would connect the bloodless bodies, sharing news through messengers, and a mob far larger than she could outrun would hunt her down. So tomorrow evening, she would make her way to the docks as soon as the last rays of light dipped below the horizon.

But first, she needed sustenance.

As the farmer's footsteps and the settling sounds of their bedtime routine faded, Niamh carefully and quietly moved through their home, slipping out into the darkness.

Unfortunately, their isolated farm lacked neighbors, and the mournful lowing of their cattle was a constant reminder that the animals were their only source of food; killing a cow would mean starvation for the couple and she would not have it.

They had been kind and she would see no harm come to them.

Yet, the surrounding forest meant wild animals, and she was desperate not to get to the level where she was no longer picky and would harm the innocent couple. Animals were not as filling as human blood, but she had little in the way of options.

The crunch of leaves and snapping twigs echoed as she walked. The forest alive with the rustle of unseen creatures, before she focused on the scurrying of larger animals, hoping to find something substantial to hold her until she could find human blood.

As if summoned by her thoughts, a deer crashed through the underbrush. Its hooves thudding on the damp earth, and Niamh was on it before it even knew she was there.

Though she hated the thought of hurting the deer, she stopped just in time, leaving the animal dazed but alive.

The metallic tang of the blood was overwhelmingly unpleasant, a stark contrast to the taste of human blood. The experience lacked the violent reaction she felt when biting a mortal male's neck.

No matter how she tried to envision animal blood when she hunted humans, it never worked. Perhaps Niamh needed to consider the new brain sciences she'd been reading about.

With a huff of amusement, she let the deer go as it got its legs under itself and took off, if a little unsteady.

The scream, a terrifying shriek that ripped through the stillness of the night, made Niamh jump as she wiped the dirt from her hands. Animals stirred, their panicked rustling and the sudden flapping of startled wings creating a cacophony that spoke of impending danger.

Despite her parched throat and the desperate need for more blood, she hurried back towards the farm. The urgency to check on her temporary landlords over-rode her gnawing discomfort and the parched dryness of her throat.

As she moved through the woods, flames erupted high into the night sky, casting an eerie orange and red glow on the surrounding trees. It illuminated the horrifying scene of the farmer's home engulfed in fire. The crackling and popping of the inferno filled the air with a terrifying symphony, and the acrid smell of smoke stung her nostrils.

Stepping out from the forest, she saw two lifeless forms lying before the farm-house and knew it could only be the farmer and his wife.

Before she could think better of it, she raced toward them, collapsing beside their still forms, her fingers searching for a pulse that was no longer there. The frozen frightened expressions on their faces spoke of a death already claimed, their eyes glazed over and lifeless. It was clear they were gone.

A sharp crack echoed through the air, sending her sprawling backward as something white and boney struck the farmer, the crimson blood welling up on the gash across his cheek.

Niamh crouched, muscles tense, her heart pounding as a familiar low chuckle replaced her instinct to fight with stark terror.

No, it couldn't be him, yet the unnerving feeling of his presence made her question reality. She had torn his head from his body herself and as far as Niamh knew, there was no coming back from that.

The heat of the fire distorted the world around her, but there was no mistaking the familiar gait of the man walking toward her.

Niamh stifled a scream as he approached; his headless body was a horrifying sight, the exposed neck a gruesome wound.

He moved closer, the dry grass crackling under his feet as embers, blown by the wind, seeded out from the burning house, spreading the fire to the high grasses of the pasture.

Frozen in fear, she didn't hear the whip's sharp crack until she felt the searing pain of the lash against her shoulder.

Biting down on her lip so as not to scream, she reached out with her hand to grab at her wound, feeling bone and thinking it was hers until it slithered away, leaving her with a fast-closing open wound.

Niamh watched in horror as a spinal cord slipped along the grass, the end in the headless man's hand as he readied another strike.

A loud neigh erupted from the horse behind him as it pounded the earth with its hooves, straining against the reins. Despite the fire in its eyes, Niamh recognized the animal.

"No, Tadhg ..." With a hushed whisper, Niamh's eyes flickered back to the headless figure, the sight of it sending a wave of dread over her. His arm rose, and a jolt of recognition shot through her as she saw his face—the once-familiar features were now etched with the wear of time, his skin like aged leather, his eyes sunken and dull. But it was the face twisted into a grotesque sneer that was the final confirmation of his identity.

"I have followed you, and you slip away into the night," the creature rasped, its rotting face a gruesome sight, and Niamh stumbled back, landing hard on the rough earth. "I told you, I am a God."

"How... how are you here?" When she finally spoke, her words were full of fear. "You... you killed these innocent people."

"You think I earned power by working hard? Demons were among us long before you were born and they promised me wealth and power, which I had until you. Only because of them, will I have the opportunity to haunt you forever, *wife*."

He'd made a deal with the Fomori. Perhaps that was why the Morrigan chose her, that she'd lived with a demon and managed to survive for as long as she did.

The monstrous face laughed, its body pulling his other arm back and slamming the spine again, almost catching her as she rolled away.

"Lady Shaw sends her regards," he laughed as he wiggled the spinal cord he was using as a whip in his hand.

His callous disregard for human life should not have shocked her since she saw his evil every time she closed her eyes. With every sip she took from a human.

She knew she had to escape, so Niamh darted to her feet, muscles tensed, ready to flee at a moment's notice. Her heart raced as she glanced at Tadhg, overcome with sadness that he had become her husband's monster, but terror won out. She shook herself and turned to her husband's grotesque face. Just seeing him again twisted her insides with terror, and Niamh knew even with her new strength, she was helpless against something made by the Fomori.

Her eyes moved over the open fields, resting on the place in the forest she had just come from and Niamh took off, running as fast as she could. Nearing the trees, she increased her pace, but the spine whip wrapped around her waist and with a sharp tug sent her sprawling onto the dirt. With a grunt, she pushed herself up, attempting to crawl away, only to feel the crushing weight of her husband's boot on her back.

Crushing her ribs, she could feel them splintering as he put more pressure on her. His hand dropped to where she could see his head from the corner of her eye. "I watched you kill those men, night after night. You are no better than me, Niamh," he said, his voice dripping with venom.

Her arms went limp as she stopped trying to fight. He was right. With each life she unknowingly took, a growing sense of despair settled over her; she could have easily died to spare those men their grim destinies, yet she continued.

His boot pushed down harder, the sound of cracking bone sharp and sickening. The sound triggered memories of the men she'd fed from, her psyche lost to the violence of her actions, her mind stuck in both the past and the present. Her mind recalled the last two murders; one victimized children, the other targeted women, mirroring her husband's brutality.

No, Niamh was nothing like him. She didn't hurt people to make herself feel taller; she went for the scum who devoured innocence.

Pushing from the ground, she tried to roll out from under his boot. "I am nothing like you!" she cried, her body bucking against his weight, but he responded by bringing his fist down hard on the back of her head. Her ears rang, her vision blurred, and a sharp pain shot through her side, as her rib settled back into place as her preternatural healing abilities kicked in.

A terrifying equine scream ripped through the air, causing her husband to lose his grip as Tadhg reared onto his hind legs. The large horse then thundered down on all fours to charge at her husband.

Now focused on the horse trying to trample him, her husband lifted his foot to get away from Tadhg and Niamh took her chance. Fear propelled her through the dense woods; branches whipped at her face and snagged her hair, but she ran, ignoring the stinging scrapes as she pushed onward.

The man that had tormented her in life was now back from the dead. All the evil and vileness of him lived on through the creature that had attacked her, and killed the kindly farmers whose only sin was taking her in.

Niamh continued until she reached the docks, then quietly boarded a ship as the sailors started their day. They would find her soon enough, but they would be out to sea, and she doubted her husband had a way of finding her now.

As everyone on deck prepared to set sail, Niamh cried over the loss of life that night. Over what had happened to Tadhg, and everything in her life that led her to that point.

The rhythmic motion of the waves soothed Niamh. It reminded her of her mother's comforting embrace as a child, and for the first time in a long while she finally rested.

Her mind calmed, and she let it wander to wherever it needed to go to heal. At the end of the long day, she knew she may have hurt people as a Dearg Due, but never in the way her husband had. His violence had not bred the same in her, and she was not the monster he was.

That night, when they found her, she paid for her passage. When the moon was high in the sky, she took a sailor to her room and fed from him. For the first time, a sense of calm washed over her, the violence of her past receding into the background.

Niamh was not a monster.

And the sailor was alive the next day to continue their voyage to a whole new life for Niamh.

Chapter 13

ONE HUNDRED AND FIFTY YEARS LATER

The air hung thick with the smells of ale and sweat as Niamh slipped into the tavern. The cacophony of shouting and clinking tankards was deafening as she threw back her hood. She moved silently to her corner booth, the worn wood cool beneath her hands, and began her nightly vigil.

Despite the ale's foul taste—a thin, watery liquid barely improved from sewage—she played her role.

This was her hunting ground. Drunk men were an easy enough target, and Niamh had followed plenty of the patrons to know there was hardly an innocent in the building.

For well over a century, she'd honed her hunting skills after leaving her homeland, but the new world presented unforeseen dangers that tested her limits. The new world was consumed by a shared paranoia, resulting in reckless actions and unwarranted blame.

Pious lot of Christians had just banned Christmas to the east of where she was, for Dagda's sake.

Each city and town she traveled through was the same. They all feared the darkness, looking for demons and witchcraft in every shadow.

Niamh even had a new name for herself; vampire. She was the *real* evil in town.

In the raucous tavern, a single innocent, amidst the throng of grasping hands, moved quickly between the tables. Her smile a mask for her discomfort as she served the swill under the watchful eyes of her father, the owner.

When the barmaid turned away, her sunny blonde hair reminded Niamh of Cae, and for a stolen moment of time, she could almost imagine her love was alive. At least until the barmaid turned back her way and a new face cut through Niamh's fantasy.

The tavern door opened, and Niamh's attention moved away from the barmaid to where her prey for the evening stalked in. A newer one to the town, fresh in from the east and well known to the church as the "judge, jury, and executioner." Placing his hat next to him on the bar, he watched the barmaid as Niamh watched him.

His gaze wasn't lustful, but held a righteous anger, as if he saw a grave injustice that demanded correction. That a woman dared to work and not stand around his house cooking game he didn't kill, as she was heavy with his spawn.

Once the drink was in his hand, he didn't do so much as pretend to bring it to his lips. When his head wasn't down, as if lost in thought, his eyes tracked the young woman as she worked throughout the evening.

Niamh was aware that his arrival spelled trouble for the barmaid. That icy knot of dread in her gut, which had never been wrong, screamed at her that he'd act before last call.

It was yet another wrong she could make right before she was called to action for the goddess.

And all she knew about when that time came, she would look nothing like she did when she'd saved Niamh, and the setting would be the gate of hell.

It was all convoluted and Niamh sometimes wondered if any of what she remembered actually happened. That this wasn't all a fever dream from some long sleep Niamh fell into. Some sickness, imprisoning her in her own mind.

The hands of the clock spun with the time they spent, him watching the barmaid, and Niamh watching him. Several times he looked out over the room, his own gut instinct most likely telling him something far more dangerous was watching.

His head fell a few times, as if he were nodding off before he shook himself and put a coin down on the bar. Taking his worn hat in hand, he placed it on his head with a long last look at the woman before he left.

Niamh was torn between following him now or waiting until the young lady was off work to make sure she made it to her bed without an issue. But she didn't have to wait long, since with a sigh, the barmaid hung her apron on the hook by the door to the kitchen. Her father only grunted in response to her goodbye from his place behind the bar. Obviously used to it and unaffected, she headed towards the back stairs leading to their small upstairs apartment.

Niamh knew the scoundrel lay in wait in the shadowy back alley, but she couldn't approach from that direction. She'd have to circle around just as he did. However, she knew she was fast enough to catch him before he acted out his crime.

The young woman's cry echoed just as Niamh cleared the corner, and there he was, his disgusting, muddy hands covering the barmaid's face to stop her from screaming again.

Pulling up the hood of her cloak, Niamh stepped forward, the man faltering as he heard the click of her boots on the pebbled ground.

"Who's there?" he asked, struggling with the barmaid.

Niamh's eyes, sharp and unwavering, tracked his every move, her silence heavy with unspoken intensity.

"Thomas, you've grown since I last saw you, and not for the better," she kept his focus on her as the woman squirmed, working to get away.

Fight harder. Niamh wished she could speak the words aloud, but she did not want the man's focus to go back to the woman.

He yelled, "Stay back!", but she stepped into the moonlight, his eyes widening in recognition. "Edward went off with you and they found him dead in a creek!"

Oh yes, Edward, who was from the church of the last town she'd been a citizen of alongside Thomas. Had a thing for hurting animals and younger boys of the town.

Niamh smiled. "You remember me then. You know that whatever you do here means you either join your friend, or you live to see another day." She tapped her lips with her index finger. "Choices, choices."

Thomas held the woman against his chest like a shield, but when the small barmaid bit down on his hand, Niamh had her advantage. Seizing the opportunity presented by Thomas' shock, Niamh cut the distance between her and him.

The rhythmic throb of the vein in his neck, a rapid pulse against his skin, drew Niamh like a moth to a flame. She felt the satisfying pop of her incisors piercing his flesh, the hot, coppery taste of his blood flooding her mouth.

With each pull, his strength waning, she braced him, her own strength growing with his decline, until finally, she let him fall, spent, into the grimy alleyway.

Normally, she'd rid the area of evidence, but she was leaving this place, and a warning to the others in the bar never hurt.

A weak exhale caught Niamh's attention, and she turned to see the barmaid on the ground. Her skin grew paler, her body weakening as blood flowed freely from her arm where she'd fallen on glass. Niamh knew enough to know that an artery had been severed.

"Oh gods," Niamh whispered as she kneeled next to the woman, her thoughts a chaotic mess as the barmaid's blood spilled onto the ground, warm and viscous.

"P-please," the woman gasped, her voice trembling with fear and exhaustion as her soft brown eyes begged Niamh to help.

Without thinking, Niamh wondered if her blood could do anything to heal the woman as it did her. She tore open her wrist, the metallic scent of blood filling the air as she placed it to the woman's mouth.

Niamh whispered, "Drink, darling," cradling the barmaid's head, yet she received no response as the woman's mouth slackened against Niamh's rapidly healing wound.

"Drink damn you!" Niamh demanded, closing the woman's mouth around her wrist, but the blood trickled out. Again, Niamh pressed her bleeding wound to the woman's lifeless lips, but the expected breath was absent; only stillness remained. The woman had passed.

"Goddess damn it!" With a raw, desperate yell, Niamh's shoulders slumped, the sound echoing in the empty space. Suddenly, the barmaid gasped, her eyes widening as her back arched dramatically off the ground, a silent scream escaping her lips before she collapsed, shallow breaths hitching in her chest.

That was enough for Niamh to think that perhaps she had saved a life for once.

Chapter 14

The woman's breathing changed, a subtle shift that stopped Niamh's knitting, the needles suspended mid-stitch. Setting aside her work, Niamh folded her hands in her lap as eyes that were red as fresh blood fluttered open.

As the woman sat up and silently took in her surroundings, Niamh could see the healthy flush grow in the woman's ivory cheeks.

With the emergence of a new immortal, a palpable shift in the balance of power, Niamh's singularity ended.

She was no longer alone, and Niamh wasn't sure how she felt about that. Cae was supposed to have been the one joining her for eternity, not a strange barmaid from a strange place.

The woman's voice was a low murmur, barely above a whisper, "I've heard of you, Dearg Due," her gaze piercing Niamh.

"Yes, but it seems we are one and the same now," Niamh responded. A knot of unease tightened in her stomach as she watched closely in case the whole situation went sideways. Though the woman didn't look at Niamh with fear as she kept her chin held high, her eyes unwavering as Niamh carefully presented a silver-backed mirror.

It was a myth, thankfully, that Niamh couldn't see herself in the mirror. Especially since she'd found the plethora of beauty choices a blessing in her immortal existence, and it would be quite difficult to put on makeup without seeing herself.

With a sigh, the barmaid pushed back her messy blonde hair—tangled and loose after the attack—and stared at her reflection in the mirror.

Niamh expected a great many things when the girl looked at herself: screaming, howling, and crying. However, she did not expect the wide smile that lit her entire countenance. "We speak of you among my small group of friends. How we would give anything to have the power to make men fear us as they do you."

A shiver of pure satisfaction ran through Niamh as she relished the compliment, the wicked trembling before her name a delicious echo in her mind.

"What do I owe?" the barmaid whispered, gathering herself, as she sat up on the old rickety wooden cot Niamh had laid her for convalescence.

Niamh opened her mouth to tell her nothing was owed, but the words caught in her throat. She tapped her finger to her lips, a thoughtful frown furrowing her brow. A long, immortal life needed a purpose, and Niamh knew that all too well since that was what drove her on the darkest of nights.

The words fell from Niamh's lips, but they felt right as she spoke them into existence.

"You will never allow someone to put their foot on your neck again. That should you see it being done to others, no matter age or gender or orientation, you will step in and save them."

"That sounds just fine." With a wide smile, the woman put her hand out. "My name is Fiona. It's nice to make your acquaintance."

Well, it looked like Niamh had made herself a friend.

Niamh found herself impressed as Fiona embraced her vampiric nature with ease. The new vampire glided through the night with an unnerving grace that took Niamh years of trial and error to achieve. Of course, Fiona had told her many tales on their long nights together hunting. How she dreamed of being the Dearg Due and used to fantasize about it falling asleep at night.

Despite Niamh's initial reservations about sharing her space and lifestyle, Niamh realized she couldn't imagine life without Fiona's ever-present, mischievous energy.

As they journeyed from town to town, the decades melting into each other like candle wax. The myth of the Dearg Due's renown grew with each passing year, a century of stories accumulating around them both like dust.

A hidden underground network had formed, and both Niamh and Fiona dedicated years to working alongside its founders, rescuing women, men, and children from harm's way. People who had found themselves nothing more than something to put under heel, just as her husband had once done to her.

Amidst the changing times, the need for a champion remained constant; unseen, Niamh, Fiona, and eventually many other women, held steadfast to their commitment. The number of vampires had increased significantly; those Niamh had given their power back to now moved freely and without fear, yet not all followed her.

Walking moonlit streets at night, the city's quiet hum a backdrop to her steps, she felt a peace from knowing she'd helped others escape harm. The afterlife offered Niamh a sense of purpose, filling her with a quiet contentment most nights, a sense of peace she hadn't known before.

But it didn't lessen the burden of the evil that had been done, and Niamh had lived through countless extremes of that.

Some nights, she longed to take giant steps, to confront the wealthy merchants whose avarice crushed the working class, but she was just one person.

Evil, corruption, greed- all of them were on every doorstep, every government, in every corner of the world.

Niamh could only take things one night at a time, and that thought was quite depressing.

She clutched her bloodstone necklace tightly. The rough texture a comfort against the harsh reality of the street scene before her: men, their faces grim, tying up their horses outside a tavern where the sounds of fighting and gambling spilled out into the street. Working women, their voices sharp and urgent, yelled from balconies, while children, clutching their mothers' skirts, hustled along.

Waiting outside one of the brothels, Niamh leaned against a wooden post, counting silently in her head. Two men fell out onto the street, pulling guns from their hips, shots going off, but only one fell to the ground, silent and no longer among the living.

Cae would have hated this place, most likely begged Niamh to find somewhere less violent, but that was the world they all had to live in to survive as creatures of the night. No respectable place would allow them to go about their business without tons of questions. And those questions quickly had the hangman's noose around their necks.

"Done," Fiona whispered as she came up behind Niamh, dabbing at her lips with a napkin, ignoring the murder they had both just witnessed.

"Under five minutes. Impressive," Niamh said as she pushed away from the post. Stepping out onto the street made of bricks, she made her way to the inn and brothel where they had procured rooms. Fiona followed quietly as they walked around the men hauling the dead body of their friend up who found himself on the wrong side of a gun.

"The world seems to grow worse and worse. Do you think it will be soon?" Fiona asked Niamh as they entered the inn, ignoring the dancing ladies and the men calling out to them. A familiar thought, a worn path in her mind, fluttered through her head as she navigated through the boisterous crowd. A brothel, teeming with life and noise, would be easy enough for them to blend in, she thought, but Fiona's question broke her away from those musings.

The same question that Niamh had herself most nights. Would the Morrigan call on her soon?

Or if the tribe of Danu could undo how hard the world had become?

Shaking her head, Niamh opened the door to their room. "We haven't seen the worst of it yet."

Not by a long shot.

Chapter 15

THREE HUNDRED AND FIFTY YEARS LATER

Niamh detested technology.

She utterly detested it.

Fighting back a scream, she pounded her fists on the desk, the jarring impact echoing the chaotic jumble of error messages assaulting her computer screen.

Every convenience designed to simplify her life only intensified her longing for a time before such inventions existed.

And the phones! The bloody incessant ringing and buzzing of phones filled the air all day, every day, a constant reminder of the overwhelming information overload that robbed people of their peace.

Her students walked through the college halls like zombies, unaware of their surroundings, bumping into each other.

It was a wonder that anything further could be done, and that humanity hadn't fallen to a standstill in their advancement. Niamh had seen empires rise and fall, land sold and bought, and the world around her grew bigger and more dizzying each decade.

But technology had become the bane of her very long existence in more ways than one. Niamh and Fiona had been caught dining out more than once via camera or phone, and had people still believed in fairy tales and monsters, they would have met the hangman's noose.

Naturally, before the ease of air travel blurred cultural lines, Niamh and Fiona had faced the noose more than once. Every time they came back to life, it was a fiery, pitchfork-filled scene.

Lost in the frustrating sea of error reports on her computer screen, her phone's insistent buzz jolted her, its light a sharp contrast to the dim office.

Grabbing it, Niamh considered throwing it across her small office but thought better of it. With a sigh, she turned it over to see Fiona's name illuminate the screen and hit the answer call button.

Fiona hated technology almost as much as Niamh did, so if she was calling, there was an emergency. Since they owned and ran a battered women's shelter, emergencies could mean lives lost.

"Fiona," Niamh greeted, but before she could continue, a bloodcurdling scream, sharp as shattered glass, erupted from the speaker, making Niamh jump back in alarm. Holding the phone away from her ear, Niamh could hear Fiona's panicked breaths.

"Fiona, darling, you need to breathe."

Even in the afterlife, Fiona was prone to fits of anxiety.

"Can you not feel it?" At last, Fiona's words spilled out, just as Niamh heard a door creak open to reveal a storm of panicked shouts, and the relentless drumbeat of many thundering feet.

Niamh stood up, looking out of her second-story college office window in the old brownstone that most likely needed to be checked everywhere for lead, but was sturdy. Through the hazy UV covering she'd installed on the glass, the world always looked muted, the sharp lines softened, and the colors washed out.

Everything seemed just as it had been every day since they'd settled in the small town.

The college was near an open plain, with mountains nestled behind it. The city, which was where Fiona was, was on the other side of the building from where Niamh was. It was a quaint, small town with just enough to support the college and its people.

Waiting, Niamh felt a building vibration, a deep hum that grew stronger, rattling the windows.

"Earthquakes do not happen here, Niamh!" With a yell into the phone, Fiona's frantic voice was barely audible over the sounds of slamming doors and girls screaming as she guided them to the safe rooms. While the women's shelter boasted above-ground safe rooms with multiple locks and security systems, a network of hidden underground tunnels provided additional emergency refuge.

Niamh had known she would need a contingency plan and that someday, the Túatha De Danann may have to do the unthinkable. She just hoped today was not that day.

The vibration intensified, rattling her travel souvenirs from their shelves, sending a cascade of trinkets and photos clattering to the floor. A gritty, dusty smell stung Niamh's nostrils as the sound of cracking plaster filled the air; she gripped her desk, the phone between her ear and shoulder as she struggled to steady herself amidst the chaos.

From the corner of her eye, a massive, inky cloud blotted out the sun, confirming her fears that the worst had happened.

"Fiona, get underground with the rest of the ladies, now!"

"We are moving below already. You'll find us? We won't last long, Niamh."

"Darling, when have I ever failed you?" Niamh asked, but her voice wavered as she dropped the phone. Even a vampire could do nothing against super volcanoes erupting.

At least the women were far enough away from lava flows. Now Niamh just needed to get herself set to rights and get to them.

Closing her eyes, she pressed the cool, smooth stone against her throat, the weight grounding her in the face of her uncertainty. When she opened her eyes, Niamh was in the veil. The world muted as the office she had been in for five years crumbled around her.

Pushing herself out of the office, she moved along with other people struggling to make it outside, able to move through them, but her steps were slow. It was difficult to stay in the place between worlds for very long.

Breaking free of the building, Niamh headed to the part of town where the shelter was. The girls could not move through the veil without her, and night was not upon them enough yet to keep them safe from the sun.

It felt like hours before the little adobe building they'd claimed as their own was in sight.

Niamh pushed through the broken door, half off the hinges from the cracked foundation, the building barely standing.

Pushing through broken furniture and dodging falling ceiling debris, the dust thick in the air, she was relieved to find the secret underground tunnel door intact. Once she was safely inside with the girls, she pulled them into the veil with her.

"What is going on?" Fiona asked, clutching the emergency radio, and listened to its crackle of static punctuated by urgent alerts of tidal waves, wildfires, volcanic eruptions, and earthquakes. It was a cacophony of natural disasters, but Niamh recognized the unnatural pattern.

It was something she knew would happen with the climate change warnings, and with the uptick in chaotic natural disasters. The guardians of humanity were losing their power and failing.

Something the Morrigan had warned her would come to pass.

"The Túatha De Danann are losing the battle."

Chapter 16

ONE HUNDRED AND SIXTY YEARS AFTER THE COLLAPSE

The veil was the only reason Niamh could keep the women with her from frying in the sun, but the sun was no longer their greatest threat.

The world around them had fallen apart the moment the Túatha De Danann had slipped into the Otherworld, leaving the earth to fall completely into Fomori hands. Or Claws. She wasn't sure since she'd never met a Fomorian before.

It was difficult to travel with so much destruction; the roads were clogged with abandoned cars, and the forested areas were breeding grounds for Fae creatures that had slipped through before the Túatha De Danann closed the veil.

Buildings were difficult to maneuver due to structural damage or humans making homes in them, willing to keep anyone out by any means.

Logically, she knew this would happen. The Morrigan had warned her that this would happen, yet nothing could have truly prepared her for the overwhelming scale of the devastation — the crumbling buildings, the fires raging, the cries of the suffering echoing through the ravaged land.

"I need to drink..." Tessa, one of the newer girls who struggled with her thirst, moaned. She had taught the girls, to the exception of Tessa since she'd only recently been turned, how to drink without killing, then how to erase the memory to keep them safe.

Something Niamh had to learn through trial and error.

Though Tessa often complained, a sharp edge to her latest words made Niamh's irritation flare. Despite their best efforts, the societal collapse resulted in widespread death, leaving them with infrequent and meager meals.

Walking through a city she could no longer recognize because of the devastation, Niamh had hoped there would be some stragglers.

Stepping over broken glass and rubble, Niamh shuddered when a slab of concrete crumbled, uncovering human remains. She was quick to lead the girls away from the corpse.

The city was a wasteland of rubble and dust. A desolate urban landscape, marked by the scars of battle: crumbling walls, pockmarked streets, and the ghostly silence of abandoned structures. Destruction, climate change, unending wars, famine, and a persistent plague had decimated the human population, leaving only scattered survivors.

There was nothing left. Just as all the other cities had been, nature had begun to reclaim the streets and buildings, with vines creeping over crumbling walls and weeds sprouting through cracked pavements.

"We are going to die, Niamh!" Tessa yelled, and Niamh hadn't realized the girl had been speaking to her still. Turning to face the eight women, her makeshift family rescued from harrowing circumstances, she knew she had to keep them safe. The weight of their survival was heavy on her shoulders.

But by all the gods was Tessa testing her patience.

"I am aware, Tessa. I have been beside you this whole time. Do not mistake my lack of words as a lack of caring!" Niamh's yell cut through the quiet, causing the girls' eyes to widen in fear. Never had Niamh lost her temper with them before.

"Look around you, Tessa darling, and tell me how I can remedy the situation to your satisfaction?"

Tessa looked away, the thick silence pressing down, a palpable weight of unspoken words and simmering emotions. Niamh was exhausted from popping them in and out of the veil as they chased shadows and had very little energy to react to Tessa's complaint nicely.

In the silence of her rebuke, a rock fell from one of the stone walls enclosing a large stately building on the very outskirts of the city, catching Niamh's attention. Standing still, Niamh held her hand up for the girls to be quiet so she could hear.

The sounds of scrambling and hushed whispers filled the air, a mix of rustling movements and urgent, barely audible voices. Niamh contemplated staying in the veil or leaving it.

But people meant blood, and Niamh pulled them from the veil now that night was upon them. It was easy enough to pull the women in but holding them there felt like a crushing weight. A tangible pressure against her mind, like trying to hold back a tidal wave. When she released her hold, Niamh felt a surge of relief, as if she had put down a boulder she'd been carrying on her back.

The women remained perfectly still, like statues carved from stone, not breathing or blinking, while Niamh checked out the situation.

A man, no, a boy on the cusp of manhood, stepped out from the darkest shadows of the night before a bright light went on, blinding her.

"We have nothing for you here," the young man said.

Oh, but he did. She could almost hear the blood pulsing through his veins.

"We are simply women looking for refuge," Niamh responded, moving to see his silhouette.

The man tilted his head, and she wondered what he thought of the nine of them. If he still saw them as a threat. "Wait, I know you..."

Unable to recall ever meeting him, she moved closer, hoping to reach him before he noticed, while he continued talking.

"You helped my sister when her husband was—"

"Michael!" Tessa's high-pitched scream cut through the quiet, making the man stumble backward before he fled toward her.

"Sis?" He was engulfed in a hug as Tessa held onto the last thread of her mortal life.

"I thought you were dead!" she cried, her tears soaking his shirt, and Niamh gave Fiona a sharp look. They had to play this carefully, but when Tessa inhaled deeply, Fiona and Niamh sprang into action, moving to break the two apart.

Niamh grabbed Tessa by the hood of her jacket, but didn't pull, instead, she used her power to compel Tessa to stop.

"You need to release your brother *now.*"

Tessa's growl was low and menacing, a sound that sent a chill down Niamh's spine, making her realize he was in grave danger. The metallic *click-clack* of rifles being loaded echoed in her ears, a sound she knew all too well.

Niamh moved forward, the pressure of her hands tightening around Tessa's neck, cutting off her breath. As she pulled her teeth out, the boy fell to the ground, his lifeless eyes staring blankly at the sky.

The scarlet blood on Tessa's hands was a horrifying sight, stark against her pale skin. A raw, primal howl, filled with anguish and despair, escaped Tessa.

She had just killed her own brother.

"Micheal!" Tessa yelled, falling to the ground next to him, shaking him as if to wake him up from sleep and not death.

Her screams brought people from their small refuge out in larger numbers. Niamh held still over Tessa as the woman tried to quell the bleeding, to no avail.

He was as good as dead the moment her fangs went in.

"Tessa, stop. You can do nothing more." Niamh ordered, keeping her eye on the humans, their fingers on their triggers.

The attack was swift and brutal. There was no warning shot, only the immediate, deafening impact of the bullet shattering Tessa's skull.

Dropping Tessa, Niamh stumbled back, a searing pain exploding in her shoulder as something hot tore through her flesh.

She'd never known a vampire to be shot in the brain, but she imagined that was the one thing Tessa couldn't come back from.

Niamh grabbed the remaining women, pushing them to run, and following behind them, though her gait was off from her injuries. She could feel bullets burning into her back and legs, but she pushed herself to run even as the pain seared through her nerves.

After spending most of the day with them in the veil, Niamh could not seem to open it again to let them back in. She was either too panicked or too tired.

As the sparse terrain stretched out around them — only scattered shrubs and exposed rock — she realized this was the last of the human settlements she knew of.

Perhaps the last opportunity for blood had just slipped through their fingers, and Niamh's slow reaction had cost them the chance to strike. The heavy silence of their small group pressed down on Niamh, a stark reminder of her failure.

As the buildings grew few and far between, they made it out of the city proper, out into an open space with little else but a few dying trees.

Collapsing to the ground, the impact jarring her already battered body, Niamh fought to regain control of her emotional state, but the searing pain made it nearly impossible.

There was nothing, and for the first time in her afterlife, Niamh felt utterly defeated.

<h1 style="text-align:center">Chapter 17</h1>

Under the watchful gaze of the full moon, Niamh led the weeping girls as their soft cries were swallowed by the seemingly endless, dark landscape.

Tessa was gone, and Niamh had to have several of the girls help her remove the bullets in her legs and back before her body healed around them. That had caused yet another breakdown of some women from violent homes.

Niamh raged internally as they continued through open terrain, the grass charred, the earth in its death throes.

She'd failed them. Had promised to protect them, and now they were starving. One was dead because Niamh didn't have the bloody insight to see that Tessa being young and untrained meant she'd kill her own brother.

If Cae had been there, she would have been the voice of reason, not letting Niamh make such ridiculous mistakes. Even after hundreds of years, the loss of Cae was a searing pain in the center of her soul. The unfairness that it was not her there alongside Niamh was just as heart wrenchingly painful as it was the day she'd laid on her grave.

Crimson stained Niamh's pale skin as her nails dug into her palms, the slick blood a cold, viscous feeling against her skin. The raw, gritty earth they traversed echoed the erosion within her.

"We cannot go on like this," Fiona said as she stepped up to walk beside Niamh. The women sniffled and shuffled behind her, a few sobs breaking through Niamh's dark thoughts here and there.

One such thought was that she should tear open the veil at dawn, letting the sun's scorching rays reduce them to ash.

"And what would you suggest, Fiona, that we lay down and let death have us?" Because Niamh was almost there, yet some brutally sadistic part of her just refused to die.

Annoying, really, that her stubbornness would lead her to continue on with the charade that she was fit to guide their little pack of misfits.

Fiona huffed, "It is always just black and white with you."

Niamh stopped, her jaw clenched tight, fists balled, the women behind them stumbling and nearly falling over each other as their mournful procession halted abruptly.

A hush fell over the crowd as the two women, their leaders, faced each other, eyes locked in a silent battle.

"Yes, Fiona, I deal in black and white, because the gray is where I found myself without choices under the control of a man who would see me dead." Looking to the rest of the women, she met each of their gazes. "You can do as you please. I will not be your savior or your warden, but if you stay, I will work to find a place suitable to survive and survive we will."

Niamh expected a response, a disagreement, but their silence and averted gazes prompted her to resume walking. This time, no one followed, and Niamh let out a frustrated huff. Days of pent-up anger escaped her in the silent, wordless release.

Goddess, she did not know what to do and could use some guidance ... and a drink.

But the truth was, they were starving, and all of them were at their worst. Niamh needed to be the one to find them a respite since she was the one who brought them onto her little immortal journey.

"We have stood at the precipice of death before, knowing that it was the easiest way out." Their stares felt like scorching brands on her back, each gaze heavy with unspoken judgment. Her words tumbled out as she struggled to maintain composure. "And yet, you each chose to fight back, not falling and letting the grave have you. You took the very power that allowed you rights and reason, and that no person would ever keep you chained again. Literally and metaphorically."

Now Niamh turned to face her little family.

"You have so much power on your own, but together, we are invincible. It is when we think ourselves weak that we have already lost the battle." Niamh felt her words saturate even the darkness in her own mind. "So, we can continue as a group or spread out and let death have us."

Silence met her as she waited for the answer. The line had been drawn in the sand.

Fiona stepped forward first, her arms crossing over her chest as she moved to stand beside Niamh and faced the women. "Well, I can't let you run off on your own. Who knows what trouble you'd find."

Niamh rolled her eyes but looked back at the six other women.

They were distraught over Tessa. Years of victimhood had heightened their sensitivity to violence, yet she also recognized their resilience.

Finally, all six remaining women stepped forward, nodding before they began walking again. Fiona took the lead as Niamh closed her eyes; thankful she didn't have to lose more of her found family.

Each of them had lived in a hell similar to her own and she would burn before she would see them lost. No, not after they fought so very hard to make it through some of the toughest battles in their lives, alone and scared.

They continued until close to dawn, the world now lacking even a mere tree or shrub. Nothing to provide cover should Niamh grow too tired to keep them in the veil.

Her concern grew when the younger ones kept falling, unable to take more than a few steps in their dehydrated states. They were far off course from where Niamh had expected, the entire ordeal with Tessa and the humans in the city throwing them in a whirlwind. Niamh knew they were no longer heading toward the coast but was unsure where their new path led.

All she knew for sure was that turning back meant certain death.

"What is that in the distance?" Fiona asked, and Niamh looked up to see a flicker of flame, its orange light dancing in the darkness.

Niamh took off from the group, the wind whipping through her hair as she ran towards the immense sandstone walls. Their sheer size breathtaking and awe-inspiring, brought tears to her eyes.

People shouted in the distance, and a few men came out from the structure with torches lit, but not to drive them away.

"Do you need help?" a voice called, and Niamh collapsed onto the dusty ground, the weariness in her bones too great to overcome.

Perhaps, they would be okay after all.

Chapter 18

FIFTEEN YEARS LATER

Modern times were all about gambling now, and Niamh felt like they had finally placed the right bet.

As people traversed the once-fertile plains, now barren desert sands, the little town that had welcomed her and her women flourished, expanding to accommodate the growing population. The sounds of hammers building new homes echoed through the growing settlement every day while Niamh and the girls remained hidden from the sun.

But Niamh knew divine intervention led them here, even though she wished for an alternate outcome for poor Tessa.

Just as she wished every night that Cae was there to walk hand in hand with her through the dark of the night and make love under the moon.

They had set up a structured government named Tanwen, and Niamh had carved out a little place in their town with the women. No one really noticed they were never out in the day, the people all around them struggling with their own new normal.

As traders came into Tanwen, they all heard stories about other towns not faring well or falling apart completely.

Entire towns, ravaged by the plague after the world's end, struggled with trade, fearing the spread of disease.

Some towns that survived the plague had lost their caravans and trade routes from fear of sickness, making their people so desperate that they had taken to cannibalism.

It was enough to make Niamh's stomach turn and for her dead heart to beat just a little faster when their own traders came back.

If they did. There were rumors of groups of people killing traders and stealing their goods, much like the highwaymen of long ago.

Niamh was happy to sit tight and live out as much time as she could in the cultural mishmash that was the sunny city of Tanwen. Adobe and sandstone buildings held all the wonders of the lost world, and plenty of the original inhabitants were peaceful sorts. Many were professors from one of the great colleges nearby.

Niamh's only fear was the growing dread of the new king, whose iron fist ruled the land after the end of the world—or the "Collapse", as the humans called it.

When they told of the dark king, all Niamh could picture was a demon in a crown. Stories of wraith-like creatures that floated and killed armies in minutes confirmed the Fomori's presence. The Túatha De Danann had left a void, and it had been filled.

Sometimes at night, Niamh would sit and think of ways to escape should the king make his move on Tanwen. They were wonderful people, peaceful, which would make it all the easier for the king to move in by force. Their words could do nothing against the sword.

Niamh wandered the streets of their home as the flickering torchlight danced on the cobblestones, highlighting the bustling groups of traders and their new goods—a welcome sight. Especially for the wee ones who danced around when given some new candy or toy and were allowed to stay up to enjoy them.

A cold wind whipped at the sheets that gave shelter from the sun during the day, and Niamh ran her hands up and down her arms.

Wandering to the fountain, one of her favorite places, she settled, letting her mind drift. Soon enough, the people would wind down for the night and she could have her supper before bed when one of them went off on their own.

"...renamed it. Was Hell's Gate."

Niamh's attention snapped to the two men unloading crates from a nearby wagon; the rhythmic thud of wood against wood punctuated their conversation.

"Sir," Niamh stood, approaching the men whose beige and cream linen trader's clothes were a blur of muted color in the dim light, their faces obscured by shadow. "You said something about Hell's Gate? What is that exactly?"

One man waved the other off and continued to work while the other stepped closer to Niamh, but not close enough to be threatening.

"A town south of here that was once called Hell's Gate is our main source of trade now that some of the other small villages fell. Some guy showed up a while back and renamed it. It's called Ifreann now."

The jolt of electricity that shot through Niamh's nervous system left her breathless, her skin tingling. Could this be what the Morrigan spoke of?

"But if you're thinking of going, do it now. Most places close up shop to outsiders when the plague hits, and it's making its rounds again."

Nodding, Niamh thanked him and stepped away, turning to where Fiona normally spent her evenings with a male that Fiona had a sexual relationship with and fed from almost exclusively. Niamh questioned her growing fondness for the male, but Fiona reassured her that they were simply friends, fulfilling each other's needs for the time being.

Before Niamh could make it to the small hut, a flash of light illuminated the alley between the small buildings used for residences.

An older woman, her skin glowing with an ethereal light that seemed to shimmer in the air, walked towards Niamh, who watched in awe, mesmerized by the sight. This woman was something ancient. Her power radiated from her, almost hot against Niamh's skin, the sand around her feet swirling gently against the older woman as she stepped forward.

"Oh, Niamh, my daughters have told me much about you."

Danu. Niamh fell to her knees, the rough ground scraping against her skin.

Her fingers brushed her skin as Danu raised Niamh's chin, the nearness of her face, the delicate curve of her jawline, taking her breath away. It was almost too much, this divine creature before her.

"Mother goddess," Niamh whispered as Danu took her hand in hers and helped Niamh to stand.

"Daughter of night, I know you are a part of the fabric of our world being woven back together after being torn so horribly, but the actions you take now could change things. We are running low on chances to get this right, so I cannot allow the same mistakes to be made this time around. I must make sure the Morrigan makes it to you alive which means no one can know about her."

Niamh nodded, knowing she would deny the mother goddess nothing.

"Good," Danu said, her hands firm on Niamh's shoulders. "Now, what do you know of a geas?"

Chapter 19

Niamh and the girls packed up that very night, leaving the next day for Ifreann.

Though she hated leaving Tanwen, the urgency in Danu's insistence that Niamh establish herself in Ifreann, coupled with Niamh's own feeling that the Morrigan was there, solidified her decision.

However, Danu also made Niamh's job a good deal more difficult. A geas, a silencing spell Danu had crafted, prevented Niamh from speaking about her purpose in Ifreann. If Niamh said something leading, the pain would be sharp, a physical ache in her chest, accompanied by a cold wave of anxiety that clawed at her insides.

She knew since she had tested it almost immediately after it was done, and Danu had to make her stop.

So now, she had to help a goddess who knew nothing of who she was, and her group could not speak of it at all to anyone but Niamh. The purpose of the geas was not given, and so Niamh was working off of blind faith. She had to put all her trust in the mother goddess that she would know when the time was right.

As Niamh shared her encounter with the goddess that evening to her friends, a palpable sense of importance filled the room. The women unanimously decided to journey to Ifreann, fully aware of the risks involved.

As the Ifreann trading group prepared to leave Tanwen the next night, Niamh decided to follow them to their new home She hoped their familiarity with the route would ensure a safe journey.

Using the veil during the day to walk behind the group, Niamh was a puddle of exhaustion and relief each night when she could drop her hold. Thankfully, they could work their magic on the men, getting sustenance before they moved back into the shadows, waiting for day to arrive.

Every morning, as the men bustled about packing up camp, their movements tense and watchful, Niamh herded her group back into the veil for another day's arduous journey.

And so it went for weeks, Niamh prayed to Danu that the town would appear soon since she was having a difficult time focusing and staying alert. In Tanwen, she'd grown so used to the freedom of not having to hide them during the day, she'd become spoiled and forgotten how tiring it was.

Behind them, the endless sandy desert stretched under a low sun, allowing them to leave the veil. A wave of excitement, punctuated by whoops and hollers, crashed over the men as they raced forward, their quickening pace kicking up a cloud of sand. Niamh, however, held her group back, waiting to see what had gotten the men riled up. Once they were far enough away, she could see the stark, imposing "Hell's Gate," etched into metal against the bleached landscape.

A bit on the nose, Niamh thought.

Niamh waited patiently, watching as the traders moved into the town before she and the women approached the gate. As they walked closer to Ifreann, her apprehension about their destination grew. The town was surrounded by a massive stone wall, its gate open, yet Niamh could sense her group's hesitation to enter.

Niamh took the lead, rolling her shoulders back to appear confident, and then crossed the gate, but her relief at moving past the first hurdle was sadly short-lived.

"Who are you?" a gruff voice rasped from the side of the main road, the words muffled by a dirty mask and shadowed cowl.

"A woman and her sisters looking for a safe place." Niamh felt a prickling unease at the sight of the man, his gaze unsettling. The way he leered, a slow, deliberate movement of his eyes, made her skin crawl with revulsion.

"No one comes in. We are dealing with enough as it is."

Well, that wouldn't do.

A younger man, tanned from the sun, with dark eyes and hair, ran up, exclaiming "Hey! Whoa..." a grin splitting his face as he approached. "Excuse the Scrios. He is the religious leadership of the church, but not the town." The younger man gave the Scrios a warning look before he turned his full attention to Niamh.

"Hello and welcome! My name is Aaron Rafferty and I am the son of the governor. Happy to help anyone in need. This your entire party?" he asked, looking past Niamh to the rest of the women.

"Yes, we have been seeking refuge after leaving Tanwen."

A low growl rumbled from the scrios in response to her words. "You cannot be considering letting these unattached women in here! Where are their menfolk?"

Aaron rolled his eyes. "I am sure that's an issue in the church, but here we are all survivors. Keep the sermons in the house of worship."

Ignoring the scrios further, Aaron waved for them to follow him as he led them into town past the gate. With her group leading the way, Niamh observed Aaron showcasing the buildings under construction, some with exposed scaffolding and the scent of sawdust hanging heavy in the air. The town was on the brink of transformation, a feeling she sensed immediately upon their arrival, the air thick with the scent of new beginnings.

Hopefully, it would be a positive change.

As she walked by, the scrios, his presence a silent threat, moved aside, but his gloved hand shot out to grasp her arm. Her fingers twitched, and she barely resisted the urge to snap her teeth at him.

"Make trouble and I'll see you walk the desert with no supplies," he said, and Niamh almost laughed.

With a sharp tug, she freed her arm, flashing a chilling smile, and fell into step behind the other women.

A prickling sensation crawled up her spine as she walked away, the weight of his gaze heavy on her back. The unsettling familiarity of the man echoed the chilling presence of her husband, a feeling that solidified Niamh's decision to keep a watchful eye on the scrios.

The town, with its weathered wooden buildings and dusty streets, evoked memories of the old west Niamh remembered from her travels. The smell of old wood and fresh mortar filled the air as men moved along the creaky scaffolding to repair the old buildings. In the distance, more men were repairing a large portion of the wall that enclosed the entirety of the town.

Aaron stopped at a large inn, its weathered timbers sagging under the weight of years and neglect.

They watched as a young man moved along the street, lighting torches and lanterns along the street as night fell around them. The sounds of construction came to a halt as the moon rose in the sky.

"This is about the only building large enough right now to hold all of you." Turning to look at Niamh, knowing she was the group's leader, he nodded toward the building. "You think it'll work?"

Niamh took in the old brick along the sides, the failing wooden porch and ratty curtains.

"We can make it work," she replied, smiling at Aaron. "Thank you for the warm welcome."

A slight glaze covered Aaron's eyes as he nodded, prompting a worried, silent exchange between Niamh and Fiona. Fiona's response was a simple, "we do what we have to do," look.

So, the warm welcome was more that Fiona was working her vampiric magic. The strain of holding it was immense; they could barely manage a few minutes, so Fiona's prolonged grip to secure their new inn meant Niamh knew she'd be collapsing in mere seconds.

"Perhaps we could set up our new home?" Niamh asked, concern etched on her face, as she moved to Fiona, gently threading her arm through Fiona's as she stumbled slightly, her knees giving way.

"Sure thing. I am about to leave town, looking for new trade routes, but you're here under my authority, so don't let anyone tell you otherwise." With a nod and a wave goodbye, he walked toward the half-finished building with the words "Sheriff's Office," crudely painted on a board above the door.

Pulling Fiona along, she was almost carrying the woman by the time the doors of the inn shut behind her.

"You fool, we could've been caught or..." Niamh went through all the horrid scenarios, but this was most likely the best possible outcome. Even if Fiona had almost killed herself using all her inner power to do so.

She'd sleep for a week if she didn't die from it first.

Placing Fiona's head gently in her lap as the girls moved around to watch in concern, Niamh took a knife to her wrist. Tilting Fiona's head up, Niamh fed her blood since there was no way of getting her a fresh meal. Not until she was mobile enough to move about in the town to hunt on her own.

When it seemed Fiona would live another day, the rest of the ladies made their way upstairs, talks of how to "doll" the place up.

Niamh sat with Fiona, gently running her fingers through Fiona's soft blonde waves, the way she would a child's, as a sense of peace settled over her. They had a home in the place she was supposed to be. Cae would have been happy for her.

It didn't mean she wouldn't give Fiona a difficult time once she woke up, but she wouldn't do it as long as she might have planned since it worked.

A knock at the door interrupted Niamh's thoughts. She placed Fiona gently on the ground before she answered, making sure no one could see her unconscious friend laying out on the ground.

She did not need to start their life here off on the wrong foot.

Niamh opened the door just enough to see the man who stood there, twisting his hat in his hands. "Sorry to bother you, ma'am, but Aaron told us some ladies were staying in the old brothel. I wanted to see if you needed anything before we went in for the night?"

Niamh almost snapped at him, but her lips stilled as an idea came to her.

"A brothel, you say?"

Chapter 20

Twenty Five Years Later

"Those blasted bells!" Fiona yelled out as she ran a cloth over the bar. "Twice a day, and it just rings on and on..."

Niamh continued to look over her inventory and the Sanctuary books, not looking up at Fiona as her friend lost herself to her temper.

It was commonplace since the plague had started to deplete their food sources once again.

"Damn doc dies and suddenly we are without a good meal!"

"We were without before he died. In case you forgot, he was trying to keep the people *alive*." Niamh turned a page as Fiona growled in response.

"If humans keep falling to this new plague, we are done for!"

"We will find some way to persevere, darling." Niamh spoke softly, trying to do calculations in her head while Fiona huffed and continued to clean the bar. They would need a trade run sooner than later since they were running out of more than just blood.

The town was declining. Even the gardens, dug deep for protection from the heat, yielded little since people were too sick to maintain them. The lack of growth there meant a significant loss of nutrients and that led to more people dying.

Not to mention the plague's gruesome effects were evident in both humans and livestock. Animals, too, succumbed to the same debilitating lethargy and swift, agonizing death.

If the humans starved, then so would she and the women she cared for.

Sighing, Niamh rubbed her eyes, knowing they would have to leave if it continued to go the way it was.

That was not something Niamh was looking to do, and not because she was supposed to meet the Morrigan here. Traders who returned from their runs spoke of several of the towns that had been decimated by the king's wraith-like assassins.

There was nothing around them anymore, the king having destroyed most of what was left. Niamh could only hope that the far east of their little piece of land had managed to hold up to the king and his machinations.

Pushing away from the table, she stood, the chair scraping against the floor, gathering her papers, knowing nothing more could be done.

They had very little coin and even less to barter with.

Times were scarce, and she truly worried for the first time since they had opened the doors to the Sanctuary in Ifreann. The Sanctuary was a place of solace and security, a haven built for the women she cherished, where they could live without fear. Though known as a brothel, the establishment was unlike others; the women weren't expected to provide sexual services. The women, instead, used their powers to secretly feed on the unsuspecting men, leaving them with the false memory of a night of intense passion.

Unfortunately, their protection was wearing thin since Aaron had left right after they had moved in and had not come back since. Too much time had passed for him to be alive, and with the governor old and feeble, she hated the idea of the pompous Scrios taking the lead.

But that was a worry for another day.

As she walked to her room, she heard the girls getting ready for the evening. The rustle of clothes and click of jewelry made her worry that the lack of recent visitors was becoming a pattern.

Ifreann was dying, and with it, any hopes of her staying long enough to know if Hell's Gate was the right place.

Defeated, she threw her papers on the desk, sat in her chair, grabbed her knitting, and began working on a new blanket. She tried to make each girl her own, and with how slow it had been, perhaps several more. Some sweaters, some scarves...

Biting down on her lip as she worked, she tasted her blood, blood that was not nearly as fresh since she hadn't had food in so long, and frustration bloomed.

She was thirsty, but when they had a client come through, she let the girls go first. Niamh refused to take anything from them.

Trying to take her mind off her thirst and the dire situation, Niamh began counting her stitches, throwing her focus into the blanket's design.

Lost to the work, she barely noticed the first pulse of the bloodstone at her neck.

Stopping her knitting, she waited, feeling a faint, rhythmic pulse restart against her chest.

With a dizzying rush, Niamh stood abruptly, the metallic clang of her falling knitting needles a stark contrast to the sudden quiet. Was this a sign?

With a crash, Niamh threw open her door, her pulse pounding in her ears as she sprinted down the echoing wooden stairs and long hallway. Her breath was the only sound cutting through the unnerving stillness of the Sanctuary.

Several girls were at the windows already, peeking through the curtains carefully, making sure the area was covered by the patio, so the sun did not hit their skin.

As she pushed her way to the window, gently moving aside the girls, she watched the guards move along the wall to raise the heavy gate.

The gate groaned open after months of stillness, and the rusty sound was almost painful, but the unspoken weight of expectation hung heavily in the air.

A gate that Niamh thought closed for good with how the scrios had enacted his orders so swiftly, going from religious leader to cult leader overnight in their small town.

The guards waiting at the gate to confirm it was their people parted, and a small group walked into the town. Their state of undress enough for Niamh to tell they were unused to the desert conditions.

In the lead was Aaron Rafferty, looking older and more worn than the bright-eyed young man who had left.

Niamh's attention moved from Aaron to a man cradling a small child in his arms.

A small girl, with red hair and fearful wide eyes curled deeper against the man's chest as people came out of buildings to watch the newcomers.

Seeing the child, a surge of fierce protectiveness washed over Niamh. She knew then that she would not allow any harm to come to the girl while she remained in her town.

A low hum from the bloodstone at her throat vibrated against her skin as she waited, breath held, for the Morrigan to walk past. When the man and child crossed where Niamh stood watching, the stone hummed ceaselessly against her chest. Niamh gasped, reaching out to grab it, the stone going inert once again at her touch.

She could barely speak from the fact that this small child was the Morrigan.

Niamh knew her debt had come due, but by the gods, she would protect that girl with her life, Morrigan or not.

Also by

Want to be the first to know about new releases, giveaways, etc.? Sign up for my newsletter!

Also By C.D. Britt:

<u>Reign of Goddesses Series</u>
Shadows and Vines (Reign of Goddesses #1)
Sirens and Leviathans (Reign of Goddesses #2)
Storms and Embers (Reign of Goddesses #3)
<u>Clan of Shadows Series</u>
Prophecy of Gods and Crows (#1)
<u>Blood of Saviors Series</u>
Reaper of Chaos (Blood of Saviors #1, Reign of Goddesses #4)
To see content before anyone else and be a part of the Reign of Goddesses community, join my Street Team on Facebook!
C.D. Britt's Legends of Halcyon

About the author

C.D. Britt has been obsessed with mythology since elementary school. That obsession has only grown, and now she pens mythology and folklore retellings, but with endings that are quite a bit happier than the original lore.

She currently resides in Texas where she has yet to adapt to the heat. Her husband thrives in it, so unfortunately, they will not be relocating to colder climates anytime soon.

Their two young children would honestly complain either way.

When she is not in her writing cave (hiding from the sun), she enjoys ignoring the world as much as her children will allow with a good book, music, and vast amounts of coffee (until it's time for wine).

C.D. Britt is the author of the *Reign of Goddesses* and the *Clan of Shadows* series.

Stay Connected!

www. authorcdbritt.com

Instagram @authorcdbritt

Facebook.com/authorcdbritt

Join C.D. Britt's Street Team on Facebook for new release information and giveaways!

Acknowledgements

This book was a labor of love created in the dark hours of the morning in November 2024. If you're a woman, you know exactly what I am talking about.

Writing this, there was so much emotional turmoil woven into the words. I worried about putting it out into the world, but I was reminded that I am not alone and many people from all different backgrounds can relate.

So, here it is, in all its angry, vengeful glory.

Thank you to everyone who shows up every day, no matter how hard it is. To my community of sisters and brothers who all stand together, no matter race, gender, how you identify, or who you love, I have a message. Stay. You are loved and meant to be here. I love you.

Katie, Jennifer, and Alyssa: thank you for being there through all of this, every day, rain or shine. I love you as if you were my family.

Paige, thank you for taking on this project at the last minute when I finally decided it might be worth a shot to throw this out in the publishing world.

Kenneth, thank you for being an amazing beta and sensitivity reader.

Brandon, you are the love of my life, and I would absolutely go feral for you. Thank you for being my equal and never trying to stand over me.

To my son, you are turning into an amazing young man. When you wrote that essay on equal rights, my mama heart was so proud of you. I have hope for the future because of you and your sister.

To my daughter, you are my little fighter who wants to right all the injustices of the world, and I know that will weigh on you. Remember to find your community and mama is always here for you.